THE VAMPIRE CIRCUS

KYLER FEY

M-BRANE PRESS

THE VAMPIRE CIRCUS

For Travis Beaudoin,
my sweet friend who was the first fellow writer who let me know
that he was a fan of my work,
which made me blush, but which also made me feel more legit...
and then he listened to me for years while I talked about writing
this vampire book...

Below lay the tomb world, the immutable cause-and-effect world of the demonic. At the median extended the layer of the human, but at any instant a man could plunge—descend as if sinking—into the hell-layer beneath. Or: he could ascend to the ethereal world above...

--From *The Three Stigmata of Palmer Eldritch* by Philip K. Dick

PREFACE

In February of 2020, just a few weeks before we knew what COVID was going to be like, I was home alone for a few days while my partner was traveling in Mexico, and I was in a deep, deep funk of writer's block and general depression related to work and life. I needed a new project upon which to focus my sluggish and undirected mind, and I couldn't find one. I had just completed the last of the ten *Commander Jace and the Unsuitable Boys* books ending a period of productivity and fun as a writer that I can't believe I ever had—fourteen published novellas and two unpublished novels in a span of four years—but everything new that I tried to start lay dead on the page already.

One afternoon, I seated myself on the couch with my laptop and printouts of various manuscript fragments arrayed about me, along with scissors and tape and high-lighters, as if I were setting myself up to get some real work done, like I was really going to have a terrific session as a Creative Writer. But what I did instead was sit there morosely and scan listlessly for stuff to watch on TV. It occurred to me that there might be Hammer Films horror movies that I hadn't seen before available for streaming, good comfort viewing for a monster kid like me. For the next few hours, that supposition was rewarded. I sat contentedly with my cats and watched the very entertaining *Twins of Evil* (1971)—part of the loosely-connected "Karnstein Trilogy" of sapphic-flavored vampire films from Hammer—followed by first-time director Robert Young's deeply weird and unexpectedly subversive film *Vampire Circus*. This movie's level of gore and nudity and eroticism is notable for a British studio film in 1972, but so, too, is the delicious depravity of the story's premise: a vampire gang comes to a small remote town specifically to murder a bunch of kids in fulfillment of a curse...and they're a traveling circus troupe for some reason.

I watched rapt and probably with a smile on my face as the most lurid, and occasionally ridiculous, vampire story I'd ever seen on film played before me, almost as if it were made just for me. I was dazzled by it. How had I never seen this before? How had I not even been aware of its existence before?

It then occurred to me that if I couldn't get any kind of momentum going on any of my stalled writing projects then perhaps I could attempt an exercise, a sort of writerly workout, by novelizing *Vampire Circus*. This project, while perhaps creatively pointless, could break through the block, I thought, by forcing me lay down a lot of words. I wouldn't have to devise my own story, characters, setting or even dialogue. All I'd need do is translate what I saw on the screen into narrative prose. This task would, I thought, exercise the torpid writerly mental muscles and loosen me up sufficiently to launch into something new. I hit PLAY on *Vampire Circus* again and took a lot of notes.

And while I did start to write something that very night,

it never, even from the first few pages, ended up being anything like the intended straightforward novelization of *Vampire Circus*. The project turned into something else almost immediately as new characters announced themselves and new situations formed in my imagination. Some of the characters in this novella have direct counterparts in the film while others do not. My story retains some of the structure of the film, most particularly in its rather long prologue that is itself almost a complete short vampire story. This mimics the film, which runs only eighty-seven minutes but has an eleven-minute pre-credits sequence set in the story's past that plays like a mini Hammer vampire movie complete with a big castle fire at the end. I happened to make this choice around the same time that the authors of Tedious Writing Twitter™ were having a seasonal spate of deploring prologues and letting everyone know how stupid they are if they write a prologue ("CuZ yOuR bOoK sHoUlD jUsT StArT wItH cHaPteR OnE!"). Reader, if you're a prologue-hater and happened to pick up this book, then brace yourself because a long-ass prologue is heading right at you, and you really do need to read it in order to understand what's going on later.

As compared to the film, I changed the vampires' approach to their mission and the methods of their evil magic while keeping their plan's utter depravity and perhaps even turning their evil up a notch. I replaced the film's lead character (played by the achingly beautiful John Moulder-Brown, who'd starred the year before in Jerzy Skolimowski's incredible film *Deep End*) with a new protagonist who finds himself much more central to the vampires' scheme than his counterpart in the film. I kept the essence of the film's incestuous acrobat siblings and gave them a big role. And, regarding them, perhaps the most sick-ass moment in the film is when they hypnotically seduce the young Hauser brothers in a hall of mirrors and kill them with fangs to their necks. This scene is deeply unsettling because it is intentionally created to have an erotic undertone, and these kids are very young, not quite even adolescents. Instead of grappling with that creepiness directly, I created a pair of characters that fill the Hauser brothers' slot but I aged them up quite a few years and made them major characters with a lot of their own hellraising agency.

And, of course, I like cats a lot. If you've seen the movie, you'll recall how one member of the circus, the sinister and seductive Emil, can shape-shift into a panther. A big black kitty gets some decent page-time here.

I hope you will enjoy my vampires and their surreal circus...

—Kyler Fey, Saint Louis August 2024

An editor's note...

You may arrive at this account of a strange set of events in a faraway land as a sophisticate from one of the modern cities of our atomic age. You may enjoy it with a sense of comfort and safety because, of course, there's no such thing as a monster who thrives on the blood and the bodies of the living to sustain its endless life. But does that concept really seem so bizarre in this current world of daily new wonders where books and films are sent by wires across the oceans and alien tripods stalk the Earth's poles for no known reason? Perhaps you will ask that same question after you have read what follows. It is the author's interpretation—with a few artistic indulgences—of a bizarre event that actually happened many years ago in remote Diaspar.

For your reference, should you wish to study this topic further, here are a few other pieces of media based upon it...

Three Bells Ring in Hell, a horror film (1922, Serbia/Prussia)

Pact of the Blood Brothers, a pornographic horror film (1931, Estonia)

Suck Me, Vampire!, an erotic horror novel by Jon St. Monocaine, (England, 1933)

Mircalla Has Risen From the Grave!, a long-running horror manga series (Japan/Canada, various writers and artists, 1941 to present)

The Adventures of Daniel Jasper, Vampire, a TV series 1947-49 British Palestine

Exhuming the Real Vampire of Diaspar, a true crime book by Josue Echevarria, Mexico 1956

PROLOGUE

THIRTY YEARS AGO...

Imagine, if you can, being *this* man on that night of swamping blood and ornate atrocity. Imagine wondering if it was all your fault. Perhaps it really *was* your fault that Juyann, your own daughter—from whom you'd estranged yourself for no good reason other than (perhaps) your own religious hypocrisy—had fallen fully in thrall to the Baron Mircalla, the lord of the Diaspar Keep, and had given herself to him fully, probably irrevocably.

And maybe it was your anxiety of guilt over this that had led you to pursue her into the moon-dappled forest that night, abandoning your motorcar next to a copse of dead hawthorn when you'd believed you'd seen her gliding like a silver-limned specter along the tree line. And maybe it was your fear for her that juddered your heart with an ache of yawning horror when you saw her pull from the thick black brush and into her long ivory arms that lanky boy Jahn, who was her younger brother and your only son who, you now knew, had been lying to you all along about shunning in prim solidarity alongside you his allegedly desecrated sister. And perhaps it was an ember of uncommon courage that lit inside you when you decided to pursue your children deeper into the night-gaunt haunted Spathe Woods, stumbling over fallen branches beneath paw-paw trees cloaked in Spanish moss, stepping in invisible puddles, flinching at the moaning growls of great potoos in the trees, knowing that every stumbling step you took brought you closer to Diaspar Keep and the depravities that the Baron Mircalla—you believed—served up to all who entered.

Is it perhaps unbelievable to think—knowing who you were then (and *always;* let's be honest)—that you actually entered Mircalla's towering mansion through the same thick copper-clad door that Juyann and Jahn had left ajar behind them? It really was just that easy. But what did you think you would see when you entered that compound of too many rooms, impossibly *large* rooms, incredibly tall walls that leaned out of the perpendicular to the travertine floors, and the gnarled wood and iron spiral staircases that led up and up and up to more and more rooms? You were little better than some stupid olden days superstitious villager intruding into the home of the lord of your province, and yet somehow—despite your gut-churned terror—you pressed forward, for some reason finally now feeling like a father to your children who were surely now lost to you, surely now fully and forever the chattel of Mircalla.

What was even going through your head when you peered over the balcony that overlooked Mircalla's gigantic cathedral-deep torch-lit bedroom suite and when you saw Juyann present her brother like a sweaty and succulent gift to the Baron? Of course you were beyond horrified as the Baron, with the help of Juyann, stripped the boy of his clothes. Jahn, for his part, seemed utterly quiescent, smiling broadly.

Had the concept of mesmerism ever come up in discussions of Mircalla's power? If it had, you would have resisted even hearing speculation about such an occult practice. Whether or not Jahn was *mesmerized* by Mircalla, you know that he put up no fight whatsoever when the Baron, a slender but muscular creature with skin that seemed to glow in the firelight of his chamber, pulled the boy's naked body to his own and kissed him, and you forced yourself to watch as the Baron assaulted your son's whole body with unspeakable carnal depravity while Juyann watched, cooing with ravening delight.

After an interminable length of this horror, you heard the Baron say to Juyann, *"One lust feeds another."* You know, because you saw it plainly, that your son smiled and laughed and felt no pain at all when Mircalla slashed the boy's ivory neck with his fanged jaws and laid it open, spraying jets of blood over the diabolical threesome. Juyann laughed, and you pretended that you did not see her join Mircalla in drinking from the blood-fountain that her brother had become.

At some point after Mircalla had finished with young Jahn and laid the boy's corpse to cool on a couch, and after Mircalla had stripped Juyann of her clothing and led her to his bed, you staggered from the mansion and somehow found your way back into the town where absolutely no one really wanted to hear what you had to say even though it had the ominous clanging ring of truth to it. The undeniable fact of so many vanished kids in the last few years had frightened even the ossified town leaders that you'd found gathered in the pub.

There you found that one fool—Mayor Quode—that

man that even *you* thought of as a throwback to medieval times. And also the drunk constable Kybo, and the drunker doctor Onsuu, and the barkeep Destrin—all of them and many others assembled as usual that night in Destrin's pub, pints in hand.

It was as if he'd missed every gruesome detail of your story when Mayor Quode—a man of truly non-descript features and affect—said with a great blanketing blandness, "But we dare not go against Mircalla. The Emperor will notice our town and send soldiers to burn it to the ground if we attack the Baron." A rumble of mumbling affirmation rolled through the pub.

But you are somewhat cheered when Destrin says, from behind his bar, "This crazy fool is just confirming for you lot what we all already knew about Mircalla anyway. But he, of all people, was somehow the only one brave enough to go see it for himself."

But the mayor: "But the Emperor!"

"Fuck the Emperor," said Destrin, a man who was loud and flamboyant by Diaspar's standards and never one to withhold his opinion on any topic. He brushed stray locks of his reddish hair away from his eyes and said, "He lives a thousand miles away and has never even heard of this dumb shit-benighted province much less our stupid little town at its ass-edge. If the great Baron Mircalla were actually some kind of lord of the Emperor's court, then why does he never leave his house? Shouldn't he, at least during some seasons, be socializing in the capital with his own kind? We could cut that bastard's head off right now and no one beyond this town would ever even know about it."

Destrin's words gained traction among the pub's patrons and somehow—you realized with renewed fright

—that your story had inspired a mob that was quickly gaining froth with the more ale that they drink.

Sooner than you'd thought possible, you were one of almost thirty men and boys—no women as they were ordered to stay behind for their protection both from violence and moral offense—who drove in a cluster of ragged and clattering motorcars to the perimeter of the Baron's mansion grounds, the dreaded Diaspar Keep. Instead of sneaking in by way of the woods like you'd done earlier, this time you'd be barging in through the front gate.

"No need to be quiet about it now," said Destrin, taking bolt cutters to the chains that held shut the towering, twisted steel gate to the great house's driveway. Metal clanged and the gate swung with a tremendous whine of corrosion and your party in their cars rolled into the front portico of Mircalla's enormous mansion.

You found yourself drawn along with the tide of the mob—now somehow armed with torches and chains and threshing clubs—as they surged toward that huge door, still ajar, and as you stepped upon the veranda, someone shouted, *"Stop!"*

Everyone turned to see Maculus, the ancient priest of the Trinity Vex church approach in halting, rickety steps, his crown of white hair standing in heaps of snarls above his brow. "It is *I* who will lead this holy mission, armed with the light of the *Lord!*" From inside his dusty cassock, he withdrew a crucifix more than half a meter in height and with a gnarled and luridly painted figure of the Christ transfixed by plastic spikes to its arms. He shook it wildly and the cross lit up, glowing from within, a baleful pale green. "We will destroy this sworn foe of our race!"

"Jesus Christ!" Destrin said and spat upon the front patio. He waved the old man and his glowing cross forward to the entrance. "By all means, Father, *please* lead the way. But bring *him* alongside you. He's the one who knows the way through the house to the Baron's suite." It is only when men shoved you forward that you realized that Destrin had meant that *you* were to be at Father Maculus's side.

It made no sense to take the stairwell that led to the balcony from where you'd watched the Baron murder Jahn and defile Juyann but that's just what you'd been about to do when a heavy wooden double-door in a dark hallway flew open and you and your mob saw Mircalla himself.

The Baron stepped toward you, clad in a sheer tunic and knee-length carmine pants. Did he avert his eerie silver eyes from the priest's glowing holy cross even a little bit? You very much doubted it. Mircalla said with a heavy tone of patrician disdain, "How do you people dare to invade my home? Do not hope that you will get away lightly with this outrageous rudeness."

The priest intoned words that you did not know: *"Strigoi! Nosferatu!"* and he pushed his glowing crucifix toward Mircalla's face. The Baron, too quickly to really clock, grabbed the cross from the priest and slammed it to the stone floor. It shattered to splinters and greenish glowing jelly spattered the area, clinging to walls and to clothes. The Baron backed away into his vast shadowy torchlit chamber and you—then as the mob leader— pressed forward, yourself pressed from behind by the others. And you saw *him* again, on that couch just as before: young Jahn naked and dead in defiled repose, his throat a gaping horror, that soft flesh torn apart by the fangs of a beast in the shape of a man. Somehow, from somewhere inside you, a roaring shout manifested, and you let it escape your mouth: *"Kill this monster now!"*

The mob pushed into the bedchamber and quickly

encircled the Baron. You saw Juyann, sheathed in blood-stained satin, and she pushed her way between two men to take her place by her master's side. Said she, "You tiny people have no idea what you've gotten yourselves into." She laughed gutturally, too low, as if emitting a voice that was not hers. You cried out when Destrin lashed her with his chain and split open the skin of her thigh, issuing a sticky ooze of dark blood.

Though Mircalla was fast and strong and took down several of his attackers, he was one against nearly two dozen and soon the lashing of chains and the strikes from clubs from all directions began to wear him down. You said, speaking so loudly again with a will you'd not known you'd possessed, "The blow must be through the heart! *Through the heart!*" Someone shoved you into Mircalla and the vampire seized your neck, opened his horror-fanged jaws and...paused. You looked down and saw just an inch away from your own chest six inches of a ragged blood-dripping stake protruding through Mircalla's. The priest fell back behind him, crumpling, as if delivering this blow had drained him of all his remaining life-force. Mircalla tottered and fell, clutching uselessly at the rod of wood that had transfixed him. He tried to climb to his knees and fell again. Juyann sobbed next to him. You saw the Baron's skin turn ashen in color and then literally to ash, and it flaked dustily away exposing a raw bloodshot layer.

An eerie scream made you spin around wildly, and you ducked as if feeling the sensation of something zipping past your head. *"I'm very hungry,"* said a boy's voice and you tipped your head back to look up and you saw that something moved in the deep darkness of the incredibly high vaulted ceiling. It skittered and clacked like an enormous chitinous insect. *"So hungry."* The shadow-thing dropped, and you screamed again, and you saw Jahn, alive again, holding one of the younger boys of the mob by his bloody neck...and lifting him from the floor, drifting upward, back to the ceiling. A sheeting rain of hot blood spattered the floor at your feet. Jahn spoke again and your breath nearly stopped. The Jahn-thing said this: *"All your children will die."* He dropped his victim to the floor and somersaulted in the air and dropped like a rock toward you. You evaded the boy's vertical lunge and Jahn lowered his feet to the floor and said it again: "All your children will die." And he stepped toward you, one more yard, and abruptly stopped, an expression of innocent surprise on his face. A crossbow bolt exited his chest from behind, and he dropped like his master to the floor. You saw the mob member with the crossbow look at you meekly, as if thinking to apologize.

Maculus, suddenly revivified, rushed to fallen Jahn and, with vials of holy water and oil in his hands, performed an abbreviated extreme unction on the already-dead boy.

But Jahn's diabolical master was not quite done speaking. In a voice that was just a scratchy phantom of how he'd sounded moments before, Mircalla, rising to his knees, said this: "That boy is right. This place is *cursed.*"

Maculus, startled, turned toward the Baron and said, "How is it that you still move and speak?" The priest brandished the cross hanging from his rosary. "It must be a powerful demon that animates this revenant." He dared step a few feet closer to Mircalla and said, "Be gone, demon! I cast you out! I abjure you from this Earth and send you to the dankest deck of Hell! Tell me your name, demon!" Maculus flung holy water at the vampire. *"Tell me your name!"*

Mircalla vomited a blast of blood at the priest, spattering his cassock, and he said one final thing: "Your children will die...*to give me back my life!*"

Mircalla fell fully to the floor and Juyann, sobbing, tried to cloak him with her own body. Men pulled her roughly from Mircalla's corpse, tearing her gown, and dragged her from the room. You and the others followed, and you were sick in your gut about what may happen to your daughter, but *was* she even your daughter anymore?

Outside the house on the vast front veranda, men threw Juyann down to the wood and three or four of them brandished and swung chains, as if they intended to beat her to death with them. That atrocity was likely exactly what the chain-men had planned but the priest Maculus got in their way. He said, "Back away, you ungodly brutes. I have the power to exorcise the demonic life-force from this helpless daughter of Christ!"

Juyann, writhing on the wood, hissed and exposed her elongated canines. She laughed in a low register not her own and you imagined that her hair turned from blonde to brick-red in an instant.

"Fuck yourself, priest!" shouted one of the chain-wielding men, and he swung at ancient Maculus, catching him across his belly. "She's already one of the filthy undead!"

It wasn't even possible anymore for you to piece together any kind of linear memory of what next ensued, but what was obvious later was that during the brawl among the men and the priest and his enemies and allies, Juyann had somehow rolled away, regained her footing and fled back into Mircalla's mansion.

You'll never reconcile what you knew of your own timid character with what you did next. It was like you'd been watching another person on TV. But you realized that

Juyann had escaped back into the house, so you somehow drew a few men of the mob who were not engaged in the brawl with the priest and told them that you needed to burn down Diaspar Keep. Some of these guys had petrol cans in the boots of their motorcars; a couple more were already wielding torches. And so, you entered Mircalla's mansion for the third time that night.

You and the others walked about spilling petrol here and there, taking care to soak anything that looked especially flammable. You decided to ignite the fire in Mircalla's bedchamber and then flee down the stairs and outside before the flames could catch up with you.

Either nobody noticed that Mircalla's staked corpse was no longer on the floor near his bed or it was just that nobody wanted to say anything about it. *You* noticed it, but nothing could have compelled you to point it out. And you turned away from Jahn's bolted body, assuring yourself that it was good that the boy's remains would become ash, purified in the conflagration.

The giant house burned incredibly hot, down to its foundation, the heat so great that even its ancient stone piers cracked, crumbled and fell once everything they were supporting had collapsed into embers and ash, and you and all the other men, and even the battered priest, eventually got back into your cars and went home. And you figured that, save for your lasting grief, it was all over.

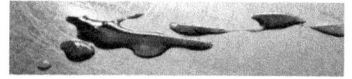

So, no one was around, then, to witness Juyann's next trial. Yes, of course, it was she who had managed to drag away Mircalla's body before the arsonists could set light to the Baron's chambers. But what if *you* had been Juyann? Well, for one thing, you'd have known somehow that the place to bring the dead vampire was deep below the house where lay in lush sunken ruin the ancient family crypt, a tiny necropolis for the Baron's ancestors, nearly choked by night-ivy and faintly lit by glowing mosses and phosphorescent moths.

Deploying strength that you'd lacked before you'd been turned into one of the undead, you'd heave Mircalla's dead weight into an open stone coffin and roll his body onto its back. Though he breathed no more, you'd find it hard to believe that he really was dead as his still-open eyes and full lips were as beautiful as they'd been in life. So, you'd let yourself stare into those unseeing eyes, willing him to somehow let you know what to do next. You may even imagine that he speaks to you from within your mind, whispering to you from the other side of this final grave. Oh, you'd strain to hear him, but the metal wind-gasps of his voice would fail to resolve into intelligible speech. And then you wouldn't hear anything at all for the next hour other than the horrendous crashing clatter of the mansion above you collapsing into burning ruins and ash. The fire above you burns so hotly that it warms even this dank cold crypt so far beneath the house's foundation.

But you need to do something *now* because Mircalla— though evidently quite dead, at least in body—seems still to look into you with that hell-gaze, as if he's been suspended in a death-liminal state, like a silver ghost bubble that you need to pop.

A dust-hazed mason jar, resting upon a lichen-crusted mortuary table, catches your eye. It's as if Mircalla had left it there *just* for you, as if he'd known already how this situation would go down for *you* specifically rather than for some random past bride. You unscrew its time-rimed lid and pull a little plastic bag from inside it. Within that age-stiff bag a starry purple galaxy-glitter of narcowhirl clings to tiny asteroids of cocaine. If you smash together this cosmic powder (as Mircalla somehow tells you to do, straight into your head from beyond his porous wall of death), then you'll be able to hear at last what he needs you to do. *If* you crush it and *if* you inhale it: a short thin osmium straw rattles like an old fossil bone in the jar's dusty bottom. You take to the marble floor with it, bare belly on stone, metal straw in your nose; and you crush and you suck and you do it *again!*

And then Mircalla, like an ambient noise at first and then like a dream voice and then, finally like a real voice in the room, tells you this:

Go to Rurimania, to the city of Transovakia, and there— once you find the Women of the Settled Hour—ask after my cousin Kasyn and his Circus of Nights. Tell them that I have sent you with a desperate mandate, which is to avenge me and to fulfill my curse upon this town. Kasyn, who may be away for many years at a time will, upon his return, immediately understand what to do once he hears my plea to him from you. The Settled Hour will guard you for as long as it takes for you to meet Kasyn. Just keep in your heart my commandment that all the children of this town must die to restore my life! That's all you need to know. Kasyn will then look into your heart and know how to proceed. Go. Now!

You rise, a revenant on marionette strings and high as kites, and find the power—through body and will and love —to plod your way out from beneath the ashen waste that covers Mircalla's tomb. Upon reaching the surface, sky lit by a low-slung blood moon, you twirl a little bit, a little private dance, because you somehow know that the stage has already been set for the circus of the vampires...

CHAPTER
ONE

P RESENT DAY...

AN ENCOUNTER IN THE CRYPT; the clouding of minds; an unusual boy's aura; Daniel senses a disturbing presence.

IT TOOK MORE than a few minutes to find the easiest access into the half-collapsed crypt beneath the ruins of Mircalla's mansion, but eventually Kasyn—a swathe of black leather and olive skin and chrome buckles and fine bones—and Magran—a tall gliding white-laced spectre—wound their way down a narrow spiral of crumbling marble steps and entered the centuries-old burial place of Kasyn's cousin and many of their ancestors.

"He lies there," Kasyn said, pointing at a hulking sarcophagus fuzzed with purple glowing night-moss. "I can smell and taste his liminal spirit, trapped in there on the wrong side of death."

Magran unpacked the pair of kerosene lamps from her tote and found flat spots among the ancient wreckage upon which to set them and light them.

"And I can smell something else, too," Kasyn added, inhaling deeply.

Magran sighed and lit a match. "And what else do you smell, aside from all this dampness and stone-rot and ash?"

"Boys." Kasyn grinned, his face now lit in yellow lamp-light. "Human boys. I smell their sick sweat and their cum and the sweet stench of their bodies. I can't say this is an *un*pleasant surprise."

Magran did a slow turn on her toes, taking in the full view of the grave chamber, now lit hotly. She could see where the chamber in which they stood opened into further chambers presumably with more ancestral remains in ranks and files of ancient death reaching back centuries. "Yes. It certainly looks like someone may have been down here recently. Do you see this?" She pointed. "And this?"

Kasyn peered at the makeshift altar littered with burnt-out candles and the stubs of cigarettes and a few empty wine bottles and an extremely ornate wooden spirit board with ebony inlays and filigrees of gold and titanium swirling about the gothic letters. "This is an antique," Kasyn said, fingering the green bottle-glass planchette, sliding it from "no" to "yes" to "maybe." He said, "I'd almost think they'd stolen it from Mircalla had the entire house above us not been burnt to ashes and slag. It looks like something my cousin would have owned. The rest of this scene, though, would be rather beneath him." He pointed at the crude graffiti, chalk-drawn on the stone walls.

Most of them were a series of necronomiconical phrases rendered in a scrawl so angular as to make them nearly illegible, but some of them were a series of crude cartoons of cocks and ballsacks, disembodied and spurting semen. "Yes, probably *boys*, as you say," said Magran. She peered more closely at the spirit board for a moment and she was startled when she heard Kasyn behind her gasp. She spun around to face him, and she saw him, hands pressed to each side of his head, stumble a bit and come to rest, back propped against the sarcophagus. "What's going on with you?"

Kasyn gasped hard, grinned, and said, "I *hear* him. My cousin! In my head!"

Intrigued by this information, Magran asked, "Can you tell me what he says?"

"Yes!" Kasyn gasped. "Listen!"

And Magran did listen, and tingles of uncanny dread prickled through her body as she watched Kasyn because his mouth did not move and he did not speak but still she heard this, in someone else's voice entirely: *"Kasyn, my cousin and sweet lover, you have come at last to avenge me. And loyal Magran, too, whom I once I knew by another name. You know what I need: the deaths of the men who slew me in the ruined house above and the blood of their children spilled over this town. They all must die to give me back my life!"*

And then Kasyn screamed and fell forward. Magran lurched for him and barely broke his fall. She assisted him into a kneeling posture on the floor next to the spirit board, and he screamed again, and tears flooded over his cheeks. "Kasyn!" Magran clasped his face tight between her palms. "Kasyn. What is happening to you? Tell me!"

Kasyn shook his head free of her grasp and laughed sharply. "My apologies, Magran. I did not expect such a...

such an *intense* reaction to the touch of Mircalla's death-suspended mental force. Not having experienced such a thing before...I guess I was quite overwhelmed by it."

Magran frowned. "Never? You mean you have never felt the touch of another's mind like that in all your long life?"

Kasyn shook his head. "Not like that. No one has ever done what we are attempting." Kasyn smiled at Magran's look of astonishment. "No one has ever resurrected a destroyed vampire."

"Never? Then how do you know—"

Kasyn pressed two fingers to her lips to shush her. "The very fact that you were able to find me with this impossible task means that Mircalla must be the most powerful ever of our kind." Magran started to speak and Kasyn shushed her again. "Listen. I hear someone."

"Someone down *here?"* Magran looked toward the collapsed entryway.

"Someone approaching. Three sets of footsteps in the tunnel. Coming down the steps. Douse the lights."

Magran shut off the lanterns and moved them into a dark corner. "Should we leave? Or do we not care if we are found in here?"

Kasyn inhaled deeply. "They won't even see us. I will cloud their minds."

Magran didn't doubt him: she'd witnessed this supremely powerful creature perform that trick many times before. She had no trouble believing that they could stand there unseen and unheard by the trio of young human males that soon emerged into the crypt, one of them carrying a galvanic lucifer, its bobbing white glow casting long shadows across the crypt. She and Kasyn moved off to the far side of the chamber, away from the altar and the sarcophagus. While they could not be seen or heard, they could still be *felt* should one of these boys bump into them.

"Look at them!" Kasyn grinned, stepping slightly closer to the trio as they paused before the altar. "Amazing!" Two of them were identical twins, obvious to Kasyn even though they had slightly differing haircuts and colors and styles of dress: the darker-haired one wore a black leather vest over a bare torso and a very short black skirt; the other wore cut-off denim shorts and a skintight shirt that looked like pink chainmail. The lighter-haired one was immaculately clean-shaven; his brother wore a bit of scruff along his jaw. One of them said, "Do you think anyone else has been down here?"

"Since the last time *we* were?" finished his brother.

"Everything *looks* the same to me," said the third boy, who stood a bit taller than the twins and seemed just slightly older, clad in a sleeveless black shirt, unruly blades of black hair falling over his forehead. Kasyn liked this one's extremely tight linen pants, so threadbare in the back as to expose a lot of the bare skin of his bulbous ass. "Looks the same but...I'm not sure."

In chorus, the twins asked, "Not sure about what?"

"Shhh." The taller boy turned slowly. "The air in here feels *weird* somehow. The smell is different somehow, too."

Kasyn stepped closer to the twins, dared to place his mouth just inches from the soft throat of the darker-haired one, teeth so close to the boy's carotid artery, *so close to that hot sweat-slicked throat ready to be opened, so close to the boy gasping and moaning under my mouth, so close to boy's super-heated blood spurting on my face like a gush of pent-up semen.* Kasyn took a deep breath, reigned in his intrusive thoughts. "Give these twins to *your* twins, Magran. Dathan and Chlora can bleed these boys out, cut their throats open in here, drain them upon out upon the sarcophagus." Kasyn clapped his hands together and grinned. "Yes, I like the symmetry of that idea even though I'd love to tear into their pretty necks myself." He reached for the boy's hair, just barely touched it with the tip of his finger, very slightly flicked at a lock of it. The boy flinched and swatted at his head, perhaps thinking a bug had landed on him.

Kasyn circled around the twins and stepped closely behind the taller boy, who was crouching near the altar, examining the talking board. He said, "Someone moved the planchette. We left it on 'no.' You're for sure you haven't been down here since the last time we were all down here together?"

The twins said no and the lighter-haired one wondered, "But who else could have been here? Who else but us even knows about this?"

Kasyn waved at Magran, asked her to come closer. "This one," said Kasyn, still looking at the back of the taller boy's neck, "is different. Can you feel it?"

Magran shook her head. "I don't feel anything."

"Well, I do. And I can *see* it! This boy is carrying a very bizarre aura with him."

Magran peered more closely. "If you say so. I don't see anything."

"No, you probably wouldn't because this is...radically different."

"In what way?"

"I see shards of black, and wisps of flame, and more black, as black as fuligin cloth, but sometimes it arcs like lightning, like hot silver or mercury against the black. And it shapes itself almost like wings that try to cloak him. It's beautiful and I have never seen anything like it." Kasyn's expression went cold, uneased. "He's extremely powerful somehow. But I can't figure it out."

"Daniel!" One of the twins reached for the taller boy's shoulder and Kasyn stepped back, dodging the kid's hand. "You're acting way too weird. What the fuck are you looking at?"

"I'm not sure." The boy called Daniel rose to his feet and turned around very slowly. Until he faced Kasyn. "Something is...*wrong* in here."

Kasyn gasped and backed up a few steps when Daniel reached toward him, and the boy's gaze seemed to fix upon Kasyn's eyes.

Magran watched Kasyn. "He can't *see* you, can he?"

Kasyn backed further away. Daniel stepped closer. "No, he can't. But he knows that someone is in here with them. He somehow *knows* it." He grasped Magran by her left wrist. "There's something dangerous and something...*out of proportion* with this one. I don't like it. Let's get out of here. Dathan and Nox are probably just about to town with the tent anyway, for our arrival tomorrow morning. We'll maybe look further into this uncanny boy later when we have more time."

As they retreated from the chamber, Kasyn heard Daniel: "I don't know what the fuck's going on. But someone *was* in here with us." Kasyn saw Daniel turn toward the crypt exit and look toward him again. "But I think they're gone now."

TWO

A tiresome meeting of the town's leaders regarding the epidemic; Destrin makes an astounding allegation; Doctor Jasper decides to act.

THIS MEETING of some of the leading citizens of Diaspar had been tedious, and most particularly so to the two relative newcomers to the town— "new" in that they'd been here less than three years, basically just since yesterday among a population that never changed other than by occasional birth and death. One of these was Elspeth Jasper, the medical doctor, a short and compactly built woman with silver-streaked black hair who emanated a palpable gravitas despite her relatively small stature. The other was Kellan Marquist, the schoolmaster, wearing his green-rimmed spectacles and the tweed jacket that he'd adopted as his uniform.

These two "scientists" as they were sometimes called, with a great sneering scorn, by some of the town's elders, were beginning to regret having requested the meeting, their purpose of which was to get Mayor Quode to finally take some kind of useful action to contain the strange illness that had besieged the population, that had started killing the oldest and the youngest of the town's citizens, that had threatened to sow terror among everyone. The doctor and the teacher stood out even further because it was only they who wore the surgical masks which they wished to promote as a means of containing the disease before it got vastly more widespread. Twice their conversation had been interrupted by the exhaust roar of the corpse van right outside the open windows of the mayor's office.

At least, thought the doctor, they had plenty of room to spread out. Quode's office was quite large with an extremely high ceiling, hung with fans and swamp coolers to keep the intense summer heat under control even with the large open windows.

"Doctor Jasper," said the Mayor, a grey man of no discernible age and a perpetual weariness of affect, "I admit that I'm not nearly as educated as you in this outré concept of invisible germs floating about and making people sick, but—as I've told you many times now—the people will not accept either the church or the school being closed to public gatherings, not for a day, not for a week and certainly not for the full month that you have proposed. And I still cannot imagine that Mister Marquist wishes to see his school shuttered either."

Kellan Marquist sighed. "And, as *I* have said many times now, I'll happily shutter the school for a while if it helps stop the spread of this disease and save some of my students."

"It ain't a *disease* that's gonna kill your students," said someone leaning against a wall behind Kellan. This was

Thom Destrin, the current pub-keeper, and the junior of the former one of the same name. "You *smart* people will probably try to shout me down, but I won't be stopped from saying what I have to say."

"Oh, Jesus Christ, Thom," said the Mayor. "Let it rest for now."

But Marquist turned to Destrin and said, "No. I want to hear this. *What* do you think will kill my students? Explain it!"

Destrin, a rather tall and lanky man, stood up even a bit taller and with great dignity, as if for once being acknowledged as having an important opinion, and he said, "Thirty years ago my father and your predecessor—" he pointed at Father Zulemus— "and you yourself, Mister Mayor-for-Life Quode, were part of a gang that slaughtered the Baron Mircalla and set fire to the Diaspar Keep which still rests in ashes and ruin up that hill. Our fathers and many men still alive to this day in Diaspar were there and took part in this horror of which none of you will speak!"

Father Zulemus, a bald man in a white cassock and wearing thick ruby-lensed sunglasses, rustled with umbrage. "My blessed predecessor protected this town for decades and he helped drive Satan himself from this land! And for that reason, we no longer speak of that devil Mircalla!"

"You don't speak of it, Father" Destrin replied, "because you're a superstitious twat of poor imagination who can't see that what these men did thirty years ago is the reason for what's happening to our town now."

Kellan said this: "What are you even talking about, Destrin? This legend about that burnt-down wreck on the hill? What can that have to do with our situation now?"

"Because," said Destrin, eyes now shimmering as if

glazed with imminent tears, "because the men that were there, the ones who slew Mircalla and burned down his mansion—including *you*, Quode, you dumb twat—heard the curse that the vampire threw down upon us as he bled out on his bedroom floor! My own father—rest his stupid soul—who encouraged the mob to form in the first place, heard it himself and it haunted him until he died. The way Mircalla told them, gasping against death, that he would live again once all the children of Diaspar have been made to die!"

Doctor Elspeth Jasper looked warily at the obviously upset publican before turning to Mayor Quode. "Mayor, *do* you have any personal insight into this lurid incident?"

Quode slumped more deeply into his desk chair. "I *was* there when the citizens put the torch to Diaspar Keep after overwhelming evidence of the Baron Mircalla's crimes against the people of this town. But I never entered the house, and I never saw Mircalla myself that night. Indeed, after the horrid incident was over with, it was *only* Destrin's father and Father Maculus who carried on for a time about this ridiculous curse." Quode paused, blinked a couple times as if being bumped on the back of his head by a new intruding thought. "Oh, yeah, there was also Damon Stukas, the man who incited the entire incident in the first place. If you are to believe what he said, his own daughter had become some kind of satanic bride to Mircalla, and she'd brought her own brother—Stukas's son—home with her as a blood-meal for the Baron. But he's been dead for many years. Passed not long after the incident, actually."

"I know I am not native to this town," Kellan said, "but you cannot live in this town for long and not hear about the legend of Mircalla's evil deeds. But surely no one—" he glanced at Destrin "—can still believe that he was a literal *vampire!* I am sure he was probably a terrible person, maybe a libertine, a decadent, perhaps a sex pervert, and quite possibly even a murderer of young people, but the undead simply do not exist. Nor do their curses."

It seemed that these people wouldn't be getting anywhere with this line of discussion, but next said Doctor Jasper, "Mayor, I don't have an opinion on this curse business, but one way or another I'm going to help the people in my care based on what I can see before my eyes and what I've learned from my lab tests. I'm going to Transovakia tomorrow, and I'll need a travel pass from you. There I can get some medicines that I believe will at least alleviate the suffering of our sick and probably end the plague altogether if it's the particular bacterial infection that I think it is."

Quode sighed and shook his head. "I was going to give you a pass a few days ago and send you off, Doctor. But it's too late for passes. They aren't honored anymore. The provincial army has thrown a cordon around Diaspar. To stop our plague from spreading beyond our town. We are completely cut off from even leaving town much less crossing the border into Transovakia."

Elspeth said with a slight smile, "I'm aware of the cordon. Give me the pass anyway. I think I have a way to get through the blockade."

THREE

T he doctor and her son initiate their daring scheme.

DIASPAR WAS A VERY small town and, as such, had certain amenities in very small supply. They only had at the most, at any given time, five or six sex workers, and currently just one of those was male. It so happened that the male one was Doctor Elspeth Jasper's son Daniel who'd done well enough at his trade to have ensconced himself in his own elegantly appointed cottage at the edge of town, just under the shadow of the hill upon which lay Mircalla's charred ruins. The boy was quite motivated to see an end to the quarantine imposed by the mysterious plague because most of his business was found with men who passed through town as tradesmen and deliverymen and random travelers. Occasionally there'd been single days when he'd sucked a dozen or more cocks in the cabs of lorries and walked away with enough money to fund his lifestyle for a few months. And so he eagerly proposed a plot to assist the doctor in breaking through the cordon and escaping to Transovakia to find a cure.

Elspeth was not, however, at all prepared to behold her son's appearance that morning. From her motorcar outside the boy's home, she watched—with a rapidly deepening degree of mortification—Daniel lock his front door and bounce cheerily toward the car in a state of what she could regard only as scandalous deshabille: the youth wore a white sleeveless tunic of a fabric so sheer as to nearly expose all of the skin of his lean and muscular torso and, below that tunic, carmine pants of such shortness that the hems rose halfway to the top of his thighs and of such a tightness that left little to the imagination. His feet were nearly bare, shod in only the most minimal transparent plastic sandals. A bright pink faux leather messenger bag hung from his bare shoulder.

"My god!" said Elspeth, as Daniel reached the passenger door. "Get in the car before anyone sees you!"

Daniel, jumping into the passenger seat, laughed. "I have no immediate neighbors, Mum. Aside from old Mircalla's ghost up there." He pointed to the hill. "And I am sure *he* has no objections to my attire. Other than, perhaps, that I wear anything at all." Daniel lit a clove cigarette and regarded his mother with a wide smile. "It is good to see you this morning, Mum, and upon the grand occasion of your brave mission to save our town!" He waved his arms and mimed a great crowd applauding and cheering.

Elspeth laughed despite herself, shook her head. "But what we are planning is really quite ethically suspect, to put it mildly— specifically in the way that you will be used in the plan—but we have to end this situation before we start running out of food around here if for no other reason." Elspeth sighed. "It is time. Though I don't want to think about it too directly, I need to know exactly what our —*your*—plan is." She started the engine and performed a cumbersome multipoint turn to steer her little Morris Minor back toward the road.

Danny unspooled the exciting plot for his mother, rolling it into Elspeth's head like a film strip:

"It's morning, and there are only ever three guards at the checkpoint this early in the day. And I *know* them quite well, you see. You'll stop the car in the brush next to the creek just before that sharp bend in the road directly before their guardhouse. I will get out and go on foot to that guardhouse. If they happen to have heard the car, I'll just tell them I got a lift from town. They will leave their post and go inside the guardhouse...with *me*, you see." Elspeth cringed and blushed. "Give me ten minutes from the time I exit the car, and I guarantee that I will have them inside and paying no attention to their duties. And they'll probably be detained for at least another thirty minutes after because what they like to do with me is—"

"That will be quite enough. *Damn,* Daniel! I do *not* need *all* the details, if you please!"

Daniel patted his mother on the shoulder. "Worry not about me, Mum. But after ten minutes have passed, start the car and resume the road and drive absolutely as fast possible past the guardhouse, where inside I will be busy with—"

"*Yes,* Daniel! I understand." Elspeth fumbled with a cigarette and a lighter. Daniel assisted her in getting it lit.

"Even if they somehow hear the car blow past, they'll scarcely care at that point because they will be deeply intent upon—"

"Truly, Daniel! I get it. You need not describe for me the

minutest specifics." Elspeth dragged on the smoke and sighed it out. "I feel like shit for agreeing to use you like this. You should have already left this stupid town for university last year, and you should not be whoring yourself to these stupid peasants. Yet here we are."

Daniel shifted in his seat, put his back to his door so that he could more directly face his mother. "They're *not* stupid peasants, Mother. They just haven't had the opportunities of education that you and I have had. I know you sometimes regret bringing us to this land, but it's done, and I am content for now. And when you talk like that about what I do to make money it makes *you* sound rather provincial. In the capital, my trade is quite respected, and you that very well."

Elspeth blushed, heated by her son's retort. "Listen to me, Daniel: I resorted to this plan *only* because the old men of Diaspar *are* so fucking stupid that they will let innocent people die of a common and easily treatable illness because they seriously believe that an old Baron that they murdered thirty years ago was a goddamned *vampire* that somehow cursed the whole town."

Daniel smiled, face shrouded briefly in cigarette smoke before it blew out the window behind his head. "*Amazing* if that were true! There's a romance to it, don't you think? A lusty vampire lord in his castle bringing savage and sexy delight to the young men and women of the town. Sometimes I fantasize that Mircalla *does* resurrect and resume his rule here, and perhaps he grabs me as one those in his immortal thrall." He paused, taking in his mother's pallor of dismay, and he added, "It's just a daydream, Mum. I mean nothing by it."

They reached their destination, and Elspeth rolled the car into a brush-choked hidden spot next to the narrow, burbling creek. Daniel reached for the door handle but Elspeth, without even planning to, reached out and pulled the boy close. Just very briefly she pressed her lips against the lad's forehead and told her son that she loved him and begged him to please be safe. Said Daniel, opening the door: "Worry not, Mum, I do this thing almost every day." Before he stepped out of the car, he opened his messenger bag and withdrew from it an envelope that he handed to Elspeth. "Deliver this for me, if you can. If you happen to see him." Elspeth looked at the inscription, stunned: *"To My Beloved Ezra."* And far as Elspeth knew, Daniel had neither seen nor corresponded with his much older half-brother in a very long time. *Why does he even think that Ezra is in Transovakia now? Why does he think I'd just happen to run into him if he were?* Elspeth had little time to contemplate it. Ten minutes were ticking by.

Elspeth didn't know, of course, that her son's daydream about Mircalla's resurrection, the one that Daniel had said meant nothing, had gone far further than a masturbation fantasy in that boy's bed. She had no idea about the repeated black masses in the moss-choked crypt, the makeshift ceremonies in which Daniel led a pair of the town's other boys in strange chants, the burning of candles and incense, the manipulation of a spirit board and the inevitable sodomy atop the sealed stone box that suppos-edly housed the remains of a vampire. This is what Daniel recalled as he approached the guardhouse: getting fucked hard on top of that coffin. It's the kind of thought that encouraged a firm erection, always good for business.

CHAPTER

FOUR

T he mayor is petitioned by the Destrin brothers; an unusual caravan arrives; an uncanny encounter with a panther.

MAYOR QUODE NEARED the end of the morning in his office. A large window was open to the street outside, which had gone blessedly quiet as everyone in the town took to their lunches or their midday naps. The death van had not rattled past at all this morning. He'd been near dozing in his chair over his paperwork—mostly death certificates for recent victims of the uncanny plague—when a loud knock had made him start to full wakefulness and "Uh, yes, come in!" he'd said, and immediately said to himself, *Oh, Jesus Christ!* as the Destrin boys—the sons of the publican— invaded his space. These shit-bird boys had been twin terrorists since at least as far back as their own christenings when they'd put out the most horrendous caterwauling when Father Zulemus had tried to rub ash on their infant foreheads and spattered them with holy water.

Without any kind of fair warning the hapless Mayor Quode was beset by Kaper and Lukan, the Destrin twins, two walking talking clothing store mannequins each somehow more fey than the other, recursively into oblivion. Though they were no longer school kids, they each wore an identical parody of their former school uniforms: white linen shirts unbuttoned to their navels, pink ties loose around their open collars, skin-tight knee length shorts of a shiny aubergine fabric. Their hair colors were slightly different—one very dark, one much lighter, both floppy, both tamed somewhat by barrettes behind their ears—but even with these slight differences, Quode really had no idea which one was Kaper and which one was Lukan. The lighter-haired one wore a darker lip gloss than the other, but that didn't help either, and they had an unnerving way of continually shifting positions as they moved, as if deliberately to further confound one as to who was who. But they'd brought to Quode a proposal and they were quite intent upon his endorsement of it.

"I don't think it can work," Quode said after a couple minutes of their presentation. "The parents, especially those of the younger children, are not likely to permit it."

"But it's a *perfect* plan!" the one that Quode had decided was Kaper adhered. "This way, the school building can be closed until the disease has passed but Mister Marquist can continue his classes out in the fresh open air! And, let's face it, a lot of the parents want to keep their kids out of the house during the day anyway, but they still love them enough to not want them to get sick and die from being cooped up in that schoolhouse."

"Why the hell do the two of you even care about the school anyway? Didn't you graduate in the spring?"

Quode noticed the one he'd decided was Lukan make a

little hand-sign at his brother, as if to communicate a secret. "Just a normal humane level concern for our community, Mister Mayor," Lukan said rather archly, with a slight toss of his head, knocking a lock of hair from in front of his eyes.

The boys' proposal was this: close the school but continue having class sessions outside in a clearing on the hill directly below the ruins of Diaspar Keep. "It's the biggest wide-open area in Diaspar," said Kaper. "Everyone can walk there, and Mister Marquist can space out all of the kids so they're far enough away from each other that they can't pass the germs."

That was about the fifth time that Kaper had rendered some version of that sentence since he and his brother had arrived, and Quode was rather tired of debating with these kids. *Yes, that's a* fine *fucking idea!* he thought. *Let's just go ahead and have school right there at Mircalla's house, bringing all the children of the town there, while half of the pinheads in this stupid town believe that it's Mircalla's curse that has brought the plague down upon us!*

But he'd been about to agree to bring up their idea for a vote at next week's council meeting just to get them out of his office when an odd clatter of jangling noise and tinkling ruckus and people's shrilling voices seemed to manifest from nowhere directly outside. People laughing, horses clomping, and a high cheery piping music overtook the place. *Is that a calliope?* Quode wondered, getting up from his desk to go to the window, Kaper and Lukan rushing ahead of him, crowding into the window, a great knot of limbs and tousled hair. Quode, using his two hands like a wedge, separated the boys and inserted himself in between them so he could see what was happening down in the street. And what he saw was this:

A procession of eight steam-vans and one horse-drawn coach had parked itself in the center of the street. All these conveyances were festooned in full rainbows of shiny fabrics and placards bearing gaudy images of wild animals —tigers, elephants, giraffes, ostriches, dinosaurs—and clowns and ballerinas. Upon the biggest of these stream-vans rode a tall brightly painted message board that read in a frothy and bubbly font: **THE CIRCUS OF NIGHTS! ONE HUNDRED DELIGHTS!** And it was indeed a calliope born upon one of the steam trucks, and now it piped out a tawdry bolero and Quode blushed to see one of the town's youths, a shirtless and unshod boy dance—or rather he was being bodily twirled—in desperate time to the urgent music by an extremely tall woman who seemed to be wrapped in a windstorm of black satiny capes and scarves that somehow left her midriff bare and terminated just above her knees. Her legs were clad in black mesh, and she laughed like chimes as she spun the town boy around another time and another time and again and finally released him as the tune ended. She bowed to him, blew a kiss at him and said, "You dance divinely, my darling!" The kid returned the bow and dashed back to his klatsch of delighted friends. Behind and above them a pair of lithe acrobats, costumed in feathers like bright macaws, leapt from one vehicle to another.

Quode had noticed the woman's vaguely eastern accent. He called down to her, "You! Gypsy woman!"

The woman looked up at Quode, frowned, perplexed, perhaps annoyed.

Said Kaper, "Don't call them 'gypsies!' That's so rude!"

"Yeah," concurred Lukan. "*So* rude!"

Quode ignored the twin irritants and said again, "Gypsy woman! How did you get past the blockade?"

The woman stepped closer to the sill of Quode's window. "Are you the burgomaster here?"

"We say 'mayor' here. But yes." Quode peered down at her, tried to get a better look into her very dark eyes. "This town has been under a provincial blockade because we are thought to have a plague afoot. No one has been able to enter or exit for the past week. You were not detained at the guardhouse? They just let you and your...troupe...pass?"

"Oh, I see!" said the woman. "We did stop at an outpost just beyond the town, that way, behind me, beside a creek." With a thumb, she pointed generally that way. "But we certainly were not detained, nor did anyone even come out to greet us. I heard myself the sounds of...men inside, but they seemed to be *busy* with something and so we just moved on."

Unbelievable! thought Quode. *This giant clattering caravan just rolled past the guard station?* He recalled—and then suppressed the recollection—the plan that Doctor Elspeth Jasper had very obliquely described to him for her own passage through the blockade to Transovakia, a sordid scheme involving the doctor's sodomite son. Which reminded him that Kaper and Lukan Destrin were rumored to cavort regularly with that depraved boy. He backed away from them as if they were suddenly filthy and said, "Go outside now. There are things to see!"

The roar of a giant cat split the air, and a muscular panther, jet as stone, came in sight within a black-wrought cage among the caravan's vehicles. The boys obeyed the Mayor and fled his office, excited to get a closer look.

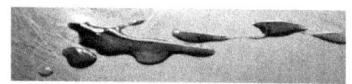

Kaper and Lukan circled the car that housed the panther, pressing amid a few of the younger children, trying to get a better look at it as the great cat hid behind straw bales within its enclosure or to take advantage of the darkness of a black curtain that covered half the cage. The calliope continued to play and behind them the so-called "gypsy woman" continued to chatter with Quode, evidently negotiating a permit for her troupe to perform in Diaspar. Kaper turned toward them and yelled, "Mayor! You simply *must* let them stay here and show us their circus!" Lukan agreed, saying into the panther cage, "It's just the thing for our depression of late!"

Then Lukan, now ignoring the noise around him, peering deeply into the panther's enclosure, saw *this* new thing in the world: the panther, like a lithe and muscular obsidian liquid, rose over a bale and—as if moving like in a slow-motion film—hopped down to the cage's straw-carpeted floor and stared, with eyes *only* for Lukan, straight *into* the boy. Perhaps captured by the cat's emerald eyes, Lukan leaned forward, unblinking, forehead against the cage's bars. The sound of his brother's voice chattering next to him at other kids receded as if drowned under deep water and he had eyes only for the panther and the panther only for him, and then...and *then*, this happened: the great cat became a man, and the most beautiful man that had Lukan had ever seen with skin nearly as black as a panther's fur and clad in a tight skin-suit of gold and obsidian that mimicked in its striped pattern the coat of a tiger, or what the panther's coat may have been had his stripes shown against the rest of his black fur. The man crept on four limbs just like a cat toward Lukan until he was so close that he nearly touched the boy's nose with his own, and he said in a dream-warped voice, *"Your brother is talking to you."*

Lukan snapped out of it, startled at the site of the great panther directly in front of him and Kaper tugging at his elbow, laughing. The cat retreated into hiding, and Lukan felt a bit dizzy as Kaper said into his ear, "The Mayor says the circus can perform three nights! They'll set up in the clearing below Diaspar Keep! We *must* go tonight! I'll suffer no objection from the Mother and the Father!"

"As *if* they could stop us," said Lukan. Though, truth be told, it would hardly be any great feat of deception for these boys to be out to a circus—or at an underground "mass" with Daniel, or anything else—in the evening and evade notice from their father Thom Destrin who would be tending to his pub or their mother who'd likely be knocked out from her evening laudanum by sunset.

CHAPTER
FIVE

A bizarre event in the woods; Daniel experiences a strange fugue.

BY UNSPOKEN UNDERSTANDING, Daniel and the trio of guards are finished with each other for the morning. The guards have fallen into sipping aquavit and inhaling rails of narcowhirl-laced cocaine. He collects his money and stuffs it into his messenger bag along with his shirt and shorts and he steps out of the guardhouse naked save for his minimal shoes. He steps into a deep rut carved into the hard-packed dirt of the road. He looks both ways and sees the tracks of some kind of large vehicle or vehicles, imprints in the dirt that were definitely not there when he'd entered the guardhouse about an hour earlier. A grip of queasiness squeezes his abdomen. His head feels fuzzed with lingering cocaine and poppers and his ass aches a little bit. Instead of walking the road, he dashes into the woods, running between trees, crouching low behind a moss-covered boulder. *What the fuck am I doing?* Suddenly feeling as if his bladder will burst, he pisses against a tree and again crouches low and runs as quickly as he can while dodging trees and jumping over fallen branches. He reaches the creek and runs into its barely shin-depth center. Obscuring his scent? Throwing them off the trail? *What am I looking for?* Warmth, blood-heat, pulses through his limbs and his dick stiffens fully even though he'd just jizzed a short while ago, made to do so in the mouth of the feyest of the three guards in the house. He thought that was good, thought that it was right with the world that boys that pretty would be good cocksuckers.

Branches crack nearby and Daniel freezes. *Who's there? How close?* He senses something move a short distance behind his back and he remains still, letting it approach. More dry crunching of leaves and snapping of twigs and then the warm loud trill of an animal very close. A purr? A growl? *A cat!* Daniel feels before he sees the tall and long and very large shape of a panther pass him on his left, prowl ahead a few paces down the bank of the creek, and then it turns back to look at Daniel. He takes a long deep breath, willing himself to be calm, and he crouches low, his knees in the water sunk in the hard clay mud of the creek bottom, his muscular calves under the clear cool water, trying to get at eye level with the creature. "Hi, kitty," he says. "Where did you come from?" The great cat creeps closer, low to the ground, eyes trained on Daniel's. It steps into the shallow water. It issues a loud snuffling purr and stops just a foot from Daniel's face. For some reason Daniel feels compelled to ask, "*Who* are you?" The panther's purr pitches lower, into a deep rumble and somehow a word comes forth from the feline sound and passes straight into

Daniel's head. *Nox,* it seems to say. *Nox,* it says again, and somehow it also asks this: A*nd* what *are you?* Daniel tries to form an answer—*a man? a boy? a faggot? horny? stupid?*— but the cat abruptly rises to its full height, turns away from Daniel and dashes off among the trees.

CHAPTER
SIX

The Destrin boys investigate the circus; an encounter with a giant; a backstage look.

As THINGS HAPPENED, as things can often happen with impulsive youths, Kaper and Lukan just couldn't wait until the actual performance that evening to get a closer look at the Circus of Nights' performers and trappings. So, barely three hours after the troupe had set off to their site below the ruins of Diaspar Keep, the twins were circling the encampment, first at a good distance but then gradually ever closer.

They crouched in brush near a back corner of what can be called the "tent" and Kaper said, "The entry to our tunnel is *inside* there!"

"Yeah, I just noticed that, too." Lukan frowned.

"It's our only way down into the crypt! What if we want to go down there and they see us?"

"I don't know. Don't worry about it now, babe."

"I wish Daniel were here now." Kaper sighed. "He would know what to do."

They'd stopped at Daniel's house on their way here hoping to induce him to come along on their reconnaissance mission, but they'd found a note that he'd be away much of the day on "business."

Lukan pulled Kaper closer, one arm tight around his shoulders. "Babe! Let's just focus on what we're doing now. Let's go in! I am sure it will be fine."

Kaper wasn't quite convinced. "But do you think they will mind us looking at their stuff before the show?"

"The worst that can happen is they ask us to leave and come back later. Besides, I'm anxious to point out to you the man that I saw in the panther cage, if indeed he even *was* a man."

"A man! Are you totally sure that you saw a *man?*"

"And a beautiful man at that. More beautiful even than Daniel."

Kaper grinned. "You've convinced me, brother. I need to see that. Let's go inside."

But before one follows the boys inside, it's worth a moment to consider exactly what they were entering. To call it a big tent doesn't quite capture it because that word suggests a much more enclosed and perhaps even a more solid structure than this thing was. Imagine instead a structure like a huge onion dome atop a Russian cathedral but it's composed of hundreds of strips of fabric in shiny gold and ruby and sapphire tones attached somehow to a gossamer lattice work, barely visible to the eye, and—my god!—it's *so* tall, perhaps the height of the Blue Mosque in the Turkish Sultan's capital and by far the tallest structure ever erected in Diaspar or anywhere in its surrounding province. If Kaper and Lukan had been even the least bit more analytical about things then they might have wondered how it had even been possible for such a thing to have been erected in the few short hours since the arrival of the Circus and, moreover, how they'd even managed to transport the vast mass of material necessary for it in their handful of vehicles, and how the very few of them had managed to do the work to get this thing built. But the boys were far from concerned with such quotidian trivia.

They approached one side of the tent more closely, not quite sure how to enter, but then a couple of the huge strips of shiny fabric seemed to separate one from the other and create a narrow door for them.

And the Destrin twins passed through that door and into an astounding cacophony of circus business: flames shot up from the center of the vast tent and someone yelled "Like this?" and someone else screamed "No! Higher!" and a tower of flame rose twice as tall and voices all around cheered and shouted. So much noise: levels of risers clattered into place evidently under the direction of a diminutive clown who shouted: "Higher! No! Higher!" and these risers somehow erected themselves in high ranks apparently by his command. Somewhere a band started a practice session, sending great thrills of drumming and pounding through the boys' guts. And then a shadow fell over them, cast by an incredibly tall and broad-shouldered man clad only in a harness and the most minimal leather shorts, a young man probably not any older than Kaper and Lukan but likely weighing at least as much as the pair of them combined. The giant said nothing, but the meaning of his body language was transparent: *Get the fuck out of here.*

But then, *"Hello!"* said a voice somehow from all around them, and Kaper and Lukan spun twice to apprehend its source but their world regained balance for a moment, and they found themselves standing in front of the dancing lady —the so-called "gypsy woman"—who'd negotiated with old Quode to perform in Diaspar. She patted the giant on one of his thick biceps. "Stand down, Jommy. They'll be no trouble." She stepped closer to the brothers and wondered, "Where did you two come from?"

Kaper opened his mouth as if to say something. Lukan stuttered uselessly. Kaper finally said, "We're very sorry to have intruded, Miss! We were just curious to see what's happening here."

The woman smiled warmly and stooped a bit to reach the twins' eye-level. "It is still a few hours until the show and we *are* very busy getting ready, but I suppose we can offer a little behind-the-scenes look for two brave boys."

SEVEN

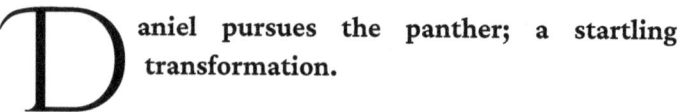

Daniel pursues the panther; a startling transformation.

DANIEL CONTINUES his way through the water. Even at the center of the creek, the water never reaches his knees. He looks down and sees a flurry of the little orange freshwater crustaceans that the locals call kudzu fish seeming to keep pace with him. *Are they tracking me? What do they want?* Straight ahead is a bend in the creek's path and there's the panther again, crouching at the bank, staring at Daniel. It rises to full height, emits a sharp roar, turns away and dashes into the brush. *He's leading me somewhere. Why?* Rationally it would make more sense to imagine the giant cat is hunting the human but playing with him for a bit before the attack. *No. I am now the hunter.* He dashes out of the water, tries to guess which way the panther ran. A rough corridor of trampled brush and leaves shows him the way. *Why am I doing this? It's fucking stupid.* Yet he persists and, sooner than he'd hoped or expected, he catches a glimpse of the beast again. He runs and, in a few moments, finds himself face to face with it. The panther sits like a contented house cat in royal repose upon a huge limestone boulder shaded by a great fall of Spanish moss that clings to the ancient tree limbs above him. It purrs, a low barely audible rumble that Daniel can feel on his skin and deep within his gut. *I guess you caught me!* Daniel whirls around, startled, wondering who said that. He faces the cat again and now its purr seems to distort into a higher-toned noise, something like a human chuckle. Again, the voice: *Let me show you something, Daniel.*

Daniel watches, wonders if it's a hallucination that he sees, because what he sees is this: the huge panther transforms, almost like a series of filmed images juddering slowly through a projector, until Daniel is certain that he sees perched upon the rock not a cat but a human male, furless save for a thick mop of jet hair crowning his head. "Neat trick, right?" says the cat-man. Daniel doesn't reply. He can't. He's forgotten how to speak. He doesn't know words anymore. He reaches slowly, cautiously, toward the man on the rock, still pretty certain that if he touches him that he will feel a cat's fur and not a human's skin. *This is not real. Not real.* The creature, whatever he is, takes Daniel's hand in his own and it feels like a normal human hand, though the fingernails are filed claw-sharp and painted a shiny black. The man who was a cat says something like, "I think *you* are the real reason we're here. I can't wait until you meet Kasyn. He'll see what I see." Daniel wants to ask what this means, wants to know who Kasyn is, but his ability to make words doesn't return quickly enough and the illusion of the strange man on the rock collapses back into the reality of the panther who bumps his hot nose against Daniel's forehead and leaps away into the deep forest.

By the time Daniel makes his way out of the woods and puts his clothes back on and completes the hike back to his house, the entire wild run into the woods and the incident with the were-panther have faded in memory and into the faintest shady film of a dream.

CHAPTER

EIGHT

The Destrin boys meet the acrobats; they are offered drugs; the encounter takes an unexpected turn.

KAPER AND LUKAN found themselves being led into the tent's depths by the lady. The giant boy Jommy followed closely and, now that he was no longer afraid of this glossy-skinned titan, Lukan wondered what it might be like to get fucked by him. *Would his cock be enormous? Could he hold me upside down by my knees and fuck my throat? Would I choke to death on his jizz? What would he do with my stupid fucking body afterward?* He returned to reality when the lady and Jommy stopped at the back of a steam van that the lady who ran the circus had called a "trailer" and said that her children are inside. "It's their dressing room. You may get to see them preparing for the show. They happen to be twins like the two of you." They followed her directions and ascended a short diamond-plate metal ramp into an open gate and through a curtain into a quite dark space.

The light seemed to raise slightly, and the boys could now see two people seated on large shiny gold and purple striped cushions on the trailer's floor with a small low glass-topped table in between them. Kaper recognized them as the acrobatic pair who who'd been performing atop the steam carts when the circus first rolled into town. They reached toward each other with tiny brushes, perhaps touching up details of each other's makeup. Little pots of face paint and powders cluttered the table. Both of them— a young man and a young woman—were entirely naked. Their intensely toned bodies were extensively inked in complex shapes and bright colors and blocks of text. The male spoke: "I'm not sure how or why, but my sister and I were somehow *expecting* you two this afternoon." He turned fully toward the boys and smiled brightly. "My name is Dathan, and this is my sister Chlora."

Chlora set down her paint brush and smiled generously. "But you cuties are rather overdressed for *this* party."

Immediately Kaper felt intensely hot. Sweat erupted over his entire body, soaking his shirt in seconds. He looked at his brother and saw that Lukan, experiencing the same thing, was pulling off his shirt. Rivulets of hot moisture dripped down Kaper's face from his suddenly sweat-sodden hair. He asked, "Should we get naked like you?"

Dathan, grinning: "We'll certainly have more fun if you do."

Kaper shed his shirt, kicked off his shoes. He watched Lukan tug down his shorts and then his jockstrap. Now, totally naked, the boys felt instant relief from the heat, and almost a chill as their sweat evaporated from their skin in seconds. They seemed to know that they were to join the circus duo at their little table, Lukan settling to his knees next to Dathan and Kaper doing the same next to Chlora.

"Feel better?" Dathan wondered. He lifted Lukan's left arm with long fingers around the bicep and pressed his nose and mouth into the still-damp hair in the boy's armpit. "Fucking delicious," he said, and Chlora concurred: "Their pheromones are insanely tasty." She licked behind Kaper's left ear.

Lukan felt hot again, but in a more pleasant way. His cock was almost painfully stiff. He noticed that Dathan's was hard, too, and clad with several cockrings—a lot like how Daniel does it—six or seven of them, alternating black rubber and red rubber and shiny chrome, matching in a way an ornate leather choker around the circus boy's neck, black and woven and trapping in its net a sparkling constellation of metallic balls and rings. Dathan's dick was quite thick with a slight curve, a hood of foreskin stretched tightly over the crown. Lukan, without really deciding to do it, lowered his lips to the circus boy's dick, lapped a drop of sticky pre-jac from its wide slit. Dathan raised Lukan's head gently by the chin and said, "We'll have time for more of that later. But first," and he pointed to the items that were somehow suddenly on the table: short metal straws, a little pile of a glittery purplish powder and tiny rocks, a vial of poppers.

"Sweet," he heard Kaper say.

"You guys ever do narcowhirl?" Chlora wondered, caressing Kaper's shoulders, wiping a new sheen of sweat from his pecs, brushing fingers over his nipples.

"We have," said Kaper. Lukan nodded, smiled. Daniel had been getting some of this drug fairly regularly from a provincial cop who passed through Diaspar weekly. He didn't even have to hand over any money for it: the cop always accepted a blowjob as payment.

Lukan said that he can't wait to tell Daniel about this

place. "Is Daniel as hot as you?" Dathan wondered, and he licked Lukan's bottom lip, pushed some spit into the boy's mouth.

"No. He's a *lot* hotter than me!"

"Then I'm going to need to know him as well as I'm about to know you. But first," and Dathan nodded toward the narcowhirl. Lukan took a straw from Dathan and saw that Chlora had given his brother one as well. They lowered their faces to the table, straws in their noses, and inhaled fat rails of the sparkling drug. Its effect was nearly instant —he felt fever-heat in his face and on his scalp and sweat erupted over his body and his cock stiffened and dripped.

Dathan unscrewed the cap from the poppers vile and raised it to Lukan's nose. The boy inhaled the vapor in a couple deep intakes and gasped at the hot blood rush in his head and in his cock. He was not near actual orgasm yet but a thick oyster of white cum wept from the wide-open slit in the head of his cock and drooled down its length. He gripped the shaft and stroked, lubing its length with slick semen. The hot rush and pump of blood in his head muffled his hearing a bit but he thought he heard Chlora say, "They are incredibly horny," and Dathan said something like, "Human boys at the height of their sexual prime—they have only one purpose in life." And the acrobat lowered his head between Lukan's legs, sheathing the boy's cock in the warm slick sleeve of his mouth and throat. Lukan looked toward Kaper and saw that the girl had gone down on him. He wondered if it had ever happened before that he and his brother had gotten their dicks sucked at the same time like this, and he couldn't recall any such occasion. But very soon, he wouldn't recall much of anything at all about this encounter. As if surfacing from a dream with no clear border between sleep and wakefulness, with no events in between, without transition, the boys found themselves outside the circus tent, walking slowly down the low hill toward Daniel's house. Said Kaper, after a couple minutes, "What just happened?"

Lukan answered, "I have *no* fucking idea." And they were overtaken by raucous laughter that did not abate for several minutes until they stepped back into Daniel's house through the back kitchen door and found that he was still not home, so they left him a note on his chalkboard. They swiped a little bud of weed from the jar in Daniel's pantry and wandered on toward their house, discussing what they might wear to the circus that night.

NINE

Daniel prepares to go to the circus; a conversation with the mayor; an astounding performance; strange encounters with two performers.

IT HAD TAKEN Daniel a few minutes to decide how to dress for the circus. He'd not even been certain that he'd felt like attending, having felt rather fagged and fashed, but he'd assumed that nearly everyone in the town would be there —it being a new thing in this small world—and, per a series of notes left on his large kitchen chalkboard by Kaper and Lukan:

"A CIRCUS has arrived. They will perform tonight just after sunset!"

"PLEASE come, Daniel! We need to know what you think of it!"

"Truly, Daniel, we're most excited and we have NO idea what to make of it!"

"***Their tent is erected upon our tunnel!*^*"

"We visited their site this afternoon, and we can't believe how much...STUFF they have!"

"Daniel, PLEASE come and look for us but do not give us TOO much attention in case Quode is watching!" [smiley face, devil-horned face]

"May we see you after the show at your house? PLEASE say YES!" [heart, heart, heart]

The note about the tent sitting over their entrance into the crypt was, more than anything else, what most interested Daniel about going to the circus. That and the fact that the troupe's encampment was basically his next-door neighbor now, and he'd hardly be able to ignore any sound or light from it whether he was in attendance or not.

He showered for a good long while, letting the hot water sooth muscles strained by his strange and barely-remembered run through the woods and rinse away the residue of sex with the guards, and eventually he felt clean and comfortable, and he dried off. He pulled the front of his hair—with the help of some stiff pomade—into a thick wave and clasped the back of it with an osmium barrette. He rubbed fingers over his chin, assessing its scruff, and decided to apply the razor. Shaving always made him horny for some reason and he considered jerking off but decided against it. If Kaper and Lukan would be here later they'd probably take care of that for him.

He put on for himself a short fashion programme in his bedroom mirror, starting with sliding several rubber and metal rings over his cock and then changing from one garment to another until finally settling upon a severe aubergine leather vest with copper buttons against his bare torso—he so very much hated to cover his arms; he'd worked so hard on their muscles—and silken knee-length pants of a silvery sheen, keeping his thick calf muscles bare, and perhaps a bit immodest since he eschewed any underwear.

Eventually Daniel decided that all this primping—after adding some eyeliner and dark purple lip gloss—had gone as far as it could go without yielding diminishing returns, and he checked the time. The show was due to start in about an hour, but it would take him less than five minutes to ascend the hill to its entrance.

So, he clicked on the radio and was unsurprised that it emitted nothing but a dull political affairs show broadcasted from the distant capital. He noted that a weeks-long stalemate was evidently still in progress as a coalition of conservative parties in the Reichstag continued to block some kind of economic anschluss with the French and the Italians. If it had been later in the evening, a radionovella that he enjoyed about a haunted mansion and its many hapless residents would have been on. He sighed and poured a finger of absinthe and lit a clove cigarette.

He tried a few more radio frequencies but found nothing of interest. A couple broadcasts seemed to be variety entertainment programs, but he could not understand well enough their languages. Another faint, crackly signal offered what sounded like a dramatic radionovella but one passing over the so-called Iron Curtain far to the east, its language fully unintelligible to Daniel. Other channels offered eerie warbles that were said to emanate from the color-out-of-space zones, also beyond the Iron Curtain.

He switched off the radio and opened the kitchen cabinet that housed his prized television set, an electrified bauble that he'd earned from a traveling salesmen with a single blowjob in the backseat of a van. He turned on the device by a stiff twist and click of a thick chrome knob and waited patiently as it took the thing a few moments to warm up and light its small ovoid screen. Often most of the several channels to which the thing could be tuned displayed either snowy static or test patterns. The technology, while not new in the world, was not yet in wide use in these parts and it seemed that it was more limited than the radio in its reach in that the source of the broadcast needed to be closer to the receiver for reasons Daniel did not quite understand. Often, when there was something to see, it might just be a dull presentation of painted aristocrats in hats dancing in a ballroom in the capital or a turgid incense-clouded church service in a cathedral, but once in a while—on no apparent schedule—Daniel would happen upon a dramatic show that always opened with strange flickering oscilloscope graphics, a synthetic musical whine and an ominous voice that said,

"*There is nothing wrong with your television set. Do not attempt to adjust the picture. We are controlling transmission. If we wish to make it louder, we will bring up the volume. If we wish to make it softer, we will tune it to a whisper. We will control the horizontal. We will control the vertical. We can roll the image, make it flutter. We can change the focus to a soft blur or sharpen it to crystal clarity. For the next hour, sit quietly and we will control all that you see and hear. We repeat: There is nothing wrong with your television set. You are about to participate in a great adventure. You are about to experience the awe and mystery which reaches from the inner mind to... The Outer Limits.*"

And this prelude was always followed by a teleplay in which strange and monstrous incursions into the normal world exposed the tattered fabric of boring old "reality." Tonight, Daniel happened to find this show right at that opening which then faded into the starkly photographed first scene of a story that the subtitle said was called

"Demon With a Glass Hand." And he was hooked into it immediately and after perhaps twenty minutes he looked at the clock and cursed the fact that it would be time to leave for the circus before the show was over.

He stubbed out his smoke and tucked a flask into his inner vest pocket as a precaution in case there were no drinks for sale at the circus, checked his clothes and hair and makeup in the mirror one more time and headed out the door.

A couple minutes later, after a short hike up the hill, Daniel passed through billowy sheer tent flaps into the astonishingly large structure. A diminutive clown at a heavy wood table took his money for a ticket and a woman clad like a moss-covered, twig-crowned forest fairy accepted his money for some sort of savory kabob meat wrapped in lacy and puffy flatbread, wet with a spicy red chutney, and a big paper cup of beer.

A makeshift stadium-style seating arrangement, consisting of a lot of benches in ascending decks looked to be nearly full. Daniel thought, *Damn. Everyone in town really is here.* He scanned about for a place to sit, hoping to find a seat on the highest level and as far away from anyone else as possible. He glanced to his left and realized that Mayor Quode and his college-age daughters Lursa and Bethel— twins like Kaper and Lukan—were seated in the front row almost directly in front of him. The moment that he made eye contact with the Mayor, Quode said, "Any word regarding your mother's mission, Master Daniel?"

Daniel was somewhat surprised that the Mayor had actually opened a conversation with him. "You'll be relieved to know, Mister Mayor, that my mother *easily* evaded the blockade and—God willing—she should be in Transovakia by now."

"Good news, indeed!" the Mayor said. The daughters, both wearing glittery black lipstick, eyed Daniel and seemed to repress giggles. He smiled and winked at them, utterly startling them, making them let loose those giggles.

Daniel bent slightly, to speak to Quode in a lower tone. "We did discuss the fact that you should try to get the telegraph in your office working again in case it's of use to receive a message that way from my mother while she is there."

Quode's expression seemed to darken, as if he'd been insulted. "We've discussed this before, Master Daniel. We are missing a replacement part and we can't get another during this blockade."

As *if* that would dissuade Daniel. Said he, "I have an intact device in my house, but it's not wired. I am sure I could help you fix yours."

But Quode adhered: "The blockade has likely cut the wires anyway. So, you see, even if my device worked, it could not receive a message."

Daniel—not wanting, as one might imagine, to waste further breath and time—said, "Enjoy the circus, Mister Mayor." He bowed slightly and added, "I'm sure we'll speak again soon."

Daniel ascended the risers through an aisle that seemed to lead to the high empty row of seating that he'd been hoping for. He winked at Kaper and Lukan—also dressed up and made up, wisps of gold leaf in Kaper's hair, silver glitter on Lukan's cheeks—who were seated in the fourth row and he nearly burst out with laughter over how the brothers glanced at him and at each other and back at him and grinned. He noticed, half-ringing the seating area from behind, a dozen tall stakes topped with what he'd thought were burning torches, but he realized that they were actually huge galvanic lucifers. Rubber-clad wires snaked down the poles, presumably connecting the bright flickering lights to power blocks somewhere below. *These circus people have really nice stuff!* he thought and decided he'd want to try to learn more about their set-up perhaps during their downtime tomorrow.

Daniel settled upon his seat and devoured his kabob and sipped his beer, and by the time he'd finished his snack it was evidently time for the show to start. The light from the galvanic lucifers lowered a few degrees and a trio of spotlights from a source that Daniel could not discern played over the stage area. *Colored gels,* Daniel thought, noting the yellow, green and pink cast to the moving circles of lights. *But where are the lights coming from?*

Next commenced a deep thumping of percussive music, but its source was not hidden: torches—ones of real flame this time—flared to either side of the stage illuminating a pair of women on one side beating large kettle drums and cymbals and a pair of men on the other side pulling long bows rapidly across the strings of a huge and strange instrument the likes of which Daniel had never seen. The drumming women wore what appeared to be skintight black body suits, and their faces were painted white whilst the stringing men wore white suits, faces painted blood-red. Soon another sound was added, the high notes from a steam calliope that contributed a comical melodic counter-argument to the stentorian drums and tense strings. Next, into the confluence of the circling spotlights stepped a little person who looked like he may have been the same clown who'd sold Daniel his ticket. This clown hopped and twirled around for a few moments, dancing to the music while a couple of black-suited stagehands positioned on the stage a trio of large clear square screens on music stands which Daniel realized were magnifying lenses when the clown stepped to the front center of the stage and his tiny painted face expanded to an enormous and watery grinning moving picture. The stagehands, who proved also to be dancers, from somewhere manifested blazing fire— sparklers on meter-long sticks—and cavorted and capered about behind the clown to the delight of children scattered through the audience. High-pitched peals of laughter pierced the volume of the vast tent. The clown, magnified by his lenses, laughed and he seemed to grip his cheeks with his white-painted fingers...and tear off his entire face. Which exposed another face beneath it, painted even more wildly, and then another. After peeling off four layers of mask, his face looked much the way it had at first, and the audience applauded. Verily, they shrieked.

Then, said the clown, voice heavy with great drama: "Ladies and gentlemen and sweet youngsters of lovely and idyllic Diaspar! Thank you all for joining us to witness *one hundred delights! The Circus of Nights!*" He bowed and twirled and the sparklers behind him seemed to double in intensity, throwing flaming cinders in a shower to the stage and the audience roared with applause. "And now!" shouted the clown, "I present to you our glorious mistress of ceremonies, the illustrious Dark Lady Magran!"

A backstage curtain directly behind the clown parted and a figure clad in a mass of dark silk arrayed upon a frame that seemed to form multiple wings glided into view and the audience seemed to inhale en masse upon the sight of her. Daniel leaned forward, fascinated. The winged woman assumed the microphone and said, "Welcome to our spectacle, my friends! Soon you will see things the likes of which you've never imagined!" A blast of firecrackers split the air, and the lucifers ringing the seating area flared briefly. "And now," she said, "watch closely and *listen* even more so!"

Daniel felt a thrill up his spine even before his ears had conveyed to his brain what he was hearing, and then what he was seeing. *Projectors!* He swiveled in his seat and saw from two makeshift platforms behind him a pair of film protectors—their clatter was what had awakened his sense-memory—beams of light aimed at a pair of stark white panels that had evidently descended somehow behind the circus stage, depending from invisible cords. A flashing, twirling countdown filled the screens...**4-3-2-1...** *A film!* Daniel nearly rose to his feet and applauded but he held back, contained somehow his thrill at seeing a thing that he'd remembered from his years in the city. Daniel thought, rather uncharitably, that these people of Diaspar had likely never seen a projected film and that they were probably the worse for it, but perhaps this experience would elevate them somehow. Daniel himself, as he would have admitted in the moment, had only seen a handful of projected films and he understood rather quickly how naïve he was in his knowledge of the medium, for what the Circus of Nights showed their audience was unlike anything that he'd imagined could even be photographed.

The mass-gasp of the audience confirmed Daniel's sense of novelty when before them on the suspended screens appeared—to the beat of drums and the whine of strings—a stark black and white montage of things flying: birds, dragonflies, perhaps dragons and possibly hovering bats; and then a total solar eclipse passed in duplicate to be replaced by shattering cracks of lightning and gales of rain, a ringed planet tumbling through space and two galaxies twisting together in silent violence, the Earth melting under a baleful nova sun.

And then a voice, but not from the film. Magran spoke: "Without further preamble, let me present the spectacle that has delighted and awed the crowned heads of Eurasia! Prepare your hearts for astounding feats surpassing even those of the supernatural and twins Phobos and Deimos— the magic of my own Dathan and Chlora!"

Daniel wondered if he should doubt his own senses when he observed this scene: twin black tornadoes seemed to form in front of the projection screens, like a three-dimensional image emerging from them. These funnel clouds descended toward the stage and slowed in their rotation until Daniel could perceive that were composed not of black storm cloud vapor but of winged creatures— two swarms of bats!

The audience gasped, confirming for Daniel that he wasn't the only one seeing it this way. Then, as the points of these bat-funnels touched the floor, the entire illusion collapsed leaving in its place two human forms, a young man and a young woman who bowed to one another, nearly brushing the crowns of their heads together. The audience clapped and gasped and screamed at the impossible materialization of Dathan and Chlora.

Daniel noticed that if he lifted his gaze just slightly, he could see the magical pair through the magnifying screens that were still in place at the front of the stage, and the sight of them—their lithe bodies and beautiful faces— gripped his attention.

Dathan, though slender, was remarkably tall and remarkably muscular in his upper body. His leaf-brown face was doll-like in its delicacy, with full scarlet-painted lips, long eyelashes and a tousled crown of unruly black hair streaked through with aubergine and silver. He wore, like the musicians, a skin-hugging body suit that left bare his calves and his belly and his arms which were either painted or tattooed with an ornate design that looked to Daniel like the script of an alien language. Rings of silver pierced the cartilage of his ears in three places each and a metal barbell passed through the upper bridge of his nose. Chlora's physical form was a feminine version of her brother's, though no less lean and muscular. Daniel wondered if perhaps she had the same tattoos but that it just wasn't possible to see them now because, unlike her brother's nearly bare body, her body suit covered everything from toes to neck and was patterned like the striped coat of a tiger, silver cat-stripes on a fuligin background, and her head was crowned with a glittering metal tiara to which huge stylized cat ears were pinned.

Drums pounded harder and strings whined louder and louder, and the twins swayed and throbbed into their act, a dance unlike anything Daniel had ever seen and which he soon understood both thrilled and scandalized the audience. Gasps and shrieks and the occasional peal of laughter from the audience punctuated the pounding music as they took in the spectacle of the twins leaping and twisting and writhing together in a bluntly erotic demonstration of their physicality and athleticism. The "story" of the dance was basically one of a lusty boy trying to tame a demonic cat-girl, trying and failing and trying again to bring her into his grasp with his long limbs and a whip, to bring her to the floor and to put her beneath his engorged crotch. She evaded his every lunge, but then seemed to succumb for a moment, allowing him to hoist her over his shoulder, but then she vaulted away, spilling him to the floor and ensnaring him with his own whip. Chlora wound it around his neck and pulled him up by it, his body twitching horribly, and then dropped him back to the floor. The music hit a sinister crescendo. *Is he dead?* A thick mist of stage-fog, lit redly from above, suddenly cloaked the pair, and they seemed to be gone. But then, as fast as the fog accumulated, it dissipated and the twins stood shoulder to shoulder and bowed deeply toward the audience. The crowd howled and laughed. Daniel felt that their mass reaction was an alloy of amazement and relief that the deeply weird dance was over and that its participants were acknowledging that it wasn't "real."

But then the duo performed a synchronized double backflip and seemed to burst into a flurry of bats that scattered to the top of the tent and vanished and the crowd fully screamed.

Daniel felt a chill and the sense of a presence very nearby. He looked to his left, startled to see who was seated next to him: *Dathan.* Said the performer, "Did you like our act? Me and my sister?" Dathan stroked the length of Daniel's arm from shoulder to wrist with hot fingers. Daniel, in that moment, wanted to ask so many things: How did you do that? How did you get here? *Who* are you? But he just stammered out a "yes" and "it was amazing."

"Watch," said Dathan, pointing down toward the stage. "If you liked what Chlora and I did, you'll fucking *freak* when you see Kasyn."

Daniel started to ask, "Who's Kasyn?" but then the man he thought he was talking to was just somehow not there anymore. He saw a lone bat bob and arc toward the apex of the tent.

The so-called Dark Lady Magran again took to the

center of the stage and spoke. "My friends, a round of applause, please, for the amazing Dathan and Chlora!" The crowd replied rather rowdily, clapping and hooting their approbation. Daniel wondered if it really was some kind magic that was teasing the raucous reaction from the usually buttoned-up and staid inhabitants of Diaspar. "And now," Magran continued, "another delight unlike any you have ever seen: Kasyn, Lord of the Cats, and his powerful and supremely deadly familiar, the panther *Nox!*"

From between backstage curtains a red light, carried by fog, flooded the floor of the stage. The curtains parted a bit more and Daniel could at first see just black forms—one of a man and one perhaps of a large animal. The black-clad man executed a triple backflip that took him nearly to the front of the stage and the animal—a gloss-black panther—leapt airborne toward him. The crowd gasped and the man ducked and rolled backward, evading the great cat's pounce. The man stood and bowed; the cat reared up on its hind legs and...seemed to bow as well, and the people applauded.

Magran again took stage-center and raised her arms levels with her shoulders. "None of what you are about to see, fine people, is an illusion. It is all real."

Daniel felt a twinge of anxiety about fire when he saw what seemed like a ball of flame, blue in its center with prominences of orange, appear a few inches away from each of Magran's hands and one about a foot above her head. A hush fell over the crowd as they watched the balls expand and then open in the center to form fiery rings, small at first but quickly increasing in size until they looked, to Daniel, perhaps a meter in diameter.

Magran receded from view and the three rings levitated in the space she'd emptied, and the band resumed its drumming and added in a new throbbing almost metallic string noise. Silent fireworks jetted from the perimeters of the stage, bloomed overhead and the panther leapt through the three rings and appeared to tackle Kasyn, but the lithe man rolled out from under the cat, tucked his head low and rose into a handstand. Nox, the panther, jumped from the floor, briefly landed on Kasyn's feet and launched himself again through the rings of fire which flared magenta upon his passage.

The crowd screamed at their next trick: Kasyn suddenly fell to his back on the floor, limbs splayed wildly, head tipped back, and the panther crept up to him, sniffed at him, circled the human a couple times and then grabbed Kasyn by the neck in his huge jaws and shook him like a limp doll and the band added shrieking strings to the pulse-beat of their drums. The horror of the crowd continued until, at last, Kasyn seemed to come back to life, work himself free of the cat's mouth, roll beneath the animal, pop up to his feet behind the beast and fling himself into a one-handed handstand on the panther's back. Nox marched in a wide circle around the stage carrying his human. And then what looked to Daniel like a surf of soot seemed flood the stage beneath the fire rings. The rings then changed their orientation, now parallel to the floor, forming a blazing column that split into six and then nine rings.

The crawling black mass on the floor seemed to be drawn upward to the fire, and then it was abruptly pulled into the fire column like a plume of smoke and ash which blasted from the top ring and congealed into a shimmering glittery cloud which quickly condensed into human-like shapes. Dathan and Chlora were back, suspended in space, and the crowd shrieked as the acrobats launched into a harrowing trapeze routine. *Where did the trapezes come from?* Daniel wondered. *What are they attached to?* More fireworks shot up from the back of the stage and a few of their sparkles lingered in the air like gently twirling stars.

Somewhere from behind the stage, a shining silver saucer-like object emerged onto the floor, carrying people. The disc was a conveyance for what Daniel soon understood was a band consisting of a guitar player and a bass player—their instruments somehow electrified—a drummer and a lead singer who swayed forward and back clutching a microphone and intoning lyrics over the band's throbbing percussive song. Daniel quickly recognized the lyrics—sung in French—as an adaptation of a Rimbaud poem but with a sinister and barely audible refrain inserted between each quatrain...

I KNEW the skies split apart by lightning!
  Spouts, breakers and tides! I knew the night!
  The Dawn exalted like a crowd of doves!
  I saw what they've seen in the light!

KILL YOUR KIDS!

I SAW THE LOW SUN, stained mystic terrors,
  Illuminate long violet coagulations,
  Like actors in a play, a play that's ancient,
  Waves rolling back their trembling shutters!

KILL YOUR KIDS!

. . .

I DREAMT the green night of blinded snows,
    A kiss lifted slow to the eyes of seas!
    The circulation of unheard-of flows,
    Sung phosphor's yellow-blue awakenings!

KILL YOUR KIDS!

FOR MONTHS ON END, I've followed the swell
    That batters at the reefs like terrified cattle,
    Not dreaming the Three Marys' shining feet
    Could muzzle with force the Ocean's hell!

KILL YOUR KIDS!

I'VE STRUCK Floridas you know beyond belief,
    Where eyes of panthers in human skins,
    Merge with the flowers beneath the seas'
    Horizon, stretched out to shadowy fins!

KILL YOUR KIDS!

I'VE SEEN the great swamps boil, and the hiss
    Where a whole whale rots among the reeds!
    Downfalls of water among tranquilities,
    Distances showering into the abyss!

. . .

KILL YOUR KIDS!

Can that be correct? Daniel shook his head. *Surely, they can't really be saying "kill your kids."* But he couldn't hear it any other way now. But the entire crowd seemed to have missed it or else they'd not be applauding so effusively. *It's at the very least a weird fucking thing to sing, right?* he thought. *If not hugely offensive.* But then he realized that possibly no one else in the crowd understood the French: *Tuez vos enfants!*

Then Daniel thought he received a second visitor in the seat next to him when suddenly sat a man that looked a lot like Kasyn but not quite. He spoke, but not quite in audible language, not quite in words but it sounded a lot like this inside Daniel's skull: "*I was his brother, and I was all but dead of a disease that an evil cleric brought onto me because of how I destroyed his god with my body. Kasyn took me to a bruja woman in the English Honduras and she saved my life, but the price is that I live most of my days in feline form. But on nights like this—magic nights! —when we perform together, Kasyn can take on my whole panther-self and let me feel life as a boy again.*" A sussurus like that of dry windblown leaves over cold paving stones underscored the panther-man's voice. "*If Kasyn loves you, you'll never die. You'll never die, Daniel!*"

CHAPTER

TEN

An eerie hall of mirrors; Daniel returns home; a quarrel with the boys.

"ARE YOU COMING INSIDE?" Daniel jolted, as if awakened from deep sleep and found himself standing in a loose queue outside a small tent. A woman waved toward the entrance. He realized it was Magran herself. *Oh yeah*...he started to remember: the show was over, but visitors were invited to see on the way out, for an additional small fee, a side attraction that they called, rather portentously, The Mirrors of Truths and Lies. He realized that he held in his left hand a paper ticket for the Mirrors. The paper was pink, and it was blurred over its surface with a stamp that looked a lot like the inky impression of a cat's paw. Magran smiled, drew herself closer to him, clasped his hand and took the ticket. She held it up and said, "I see that Nox has given you a complimentary ticket to the Mirrors."

You mean that was *real?* Daniel wanted to say but he

didn't. Instead, he quietly passed through the entrance and was startled by sudden raucous laughter. Mayor Quode was a few people ahead of him in line, paused at a mirror which, as far as Daniel could tell from his vantage point, wildly distorted his image, elongating it and turning into a zigzag. This was evidently the most hilarious thing that the man had ever encountered in his life as he nearly doubled over, all but fatally overcome by rib-straining mirth. Progress through the little hall of mirrors was rather slow: there were six mirrors and Mayor Quode was thrown into lengthy paroxysms of laughter at each one, and Daniel wondered that the man did not expire from the strain.

In the first mirror, Daniel saw himself in the same way that he assumed that the Mayor saw himself—zig-zagged with a huge jack-in-the-box head—but he didn't find it all that comical. *Perhaps you had to be there,* he thought. And then laughed at his own internal quip. But he didn't laugh at the image in the second mirror: he looked fairly normal, but he seemed to wear the panther Nox like a cloak, the great cat's head resting atop his own, panther arms reaching down the lengths of his own arms, covering his hands in huge black paws. He shook his head and the illusion vanished, leaving just his own normal-looking reflection. The third mirror made him look compressed, as if he were a tin toy man that had been flattened from head downward by a foot. He thought he saw Kaper and Lukan behind him for a moment, but when he turned to see them, they weren't there. A youth that he didn't know looked at him quizzically, as if to say, "You ever gonna move, brother?"

The fourth mirror showed Daniel a reasonably normal image, though he seemed to be limned in a solar corona and behind him fluttered a gang of bats. He didn't turn around to look behind him this time. He stepped quickly to the fifth mirror which presented his image polarized as if he were seeing the film negative from a camera. And again, something approached from behind: Dathan and Chlora flanked him, and Dathan seemed to whisper into Daniel's ear *"You wanna see how we do our tricks?"*

Daniel closed his eyes and said to himself, "It's not real. Not real." He opened his eyes and the illusion was gone. Eager to leave, he turned toward the exit at the back of the tent and was confronted by the sixth and final mirror. In a silvery field of swimming glass, Daniel saw this: himself clad in black leather and rubber and enmeshed in a harness and cables and chains, with a huge cloak reaching away from his shoulders and above his head when he extended his arms. But Daniel was not extending his arms. His image moved independently, and it leaned its pallid face toward Daniel. He could smell his doppelgänger, the sweat under the leather, the dampness of his hair. The Daniel-thing grinned, its wide mouth a horror of canine teeth and blood. It said, *"You'll never die, Daniel!"*

DANIEL DIDN'T REALLY REMEMBER LEAVING the hall of mirrors. He came back to full awareness of his surroundings as he neared his own kitchen door. More light shone through the windows than he had left on. *Fuck,* he thought. *I forgot about them.* He recalled the notes that the twins had left on the board in his kitchen. Kaper and Lukan had preceded him here. He wasn't in the greatest mood for company. He opened the kitchen door and a waft of weed smoked hit him. He heard one boy cough and another laugh. They seemed to not notice his entrance at first. Lukan perched in a crouch on a bar stool, naked save for his briefs, a puddle of clothes on the floor beneath him. Kaper sat bare-assed on the counter next to the sink, wearing a sheer silver button-down shirt and nothing else. He was about to apply flame to his bat-hitter when he noticed Daniel in the room. He shrieked, "Daniel!" and his brother stood fully on the stool and said, "We'd wondered if you'd *ever* be back!"

Daniel opened the refrigerator, withdrew a partial bottle of white wine and gulped from it. Kaper asked him if he'd had a trick after the show and is that why he was so long getting home. Daniel shook his head, gulped some more wine, and said, "I was delayed because I went into that mirrors attraction that they have near the exit."

"What mirrors attraction?" Kaper wondered.

Lukan knew. "You know. That thing I wanted to check out but you didn't want to waste the time and money. Perhaps we shall go tomorrow, though."

Lukan had resumed his crouch on the stool, smiling at Daniel. Who suddenly seemed to *float* across the floor and grab the boy off the stool, lift him fully and pin him, his back against a wall, his feet kicking a meter from the floor. "*No!*" Daniel shouted. "*You will not see those mirrors!*"

Kaper, as if to come his brother's rescue, jumped off the counter and clasped both hands hard around Daniel's left arm. "Let him down! Jesus *fuck*, Daniel! What the hell's going on with you?"

Daniel shrugged out of Kaper's grip, lowered Lukan's feet to the floor and released him. He backed away from Lukan and rubbed his eyes with both fists. "Oh my god. I'm so sorry. I don't know why I did that. I really don't. I just...I just don't want you going in there. You need to *please* promise me that you won't."

Kaper: "Not promising *shit* until you explain this."

Lukan smirked. "As *if* I'm gonna promise you anything now that you've intrigued me so."

"I'm not fucking around, Lukan." Daniel clasped his hands over his head as if trying to keep something either in or out. "I'm sorry I'm acting this way but I am seriously asking you to listen to me and to make this promise to me."

Kaper pulled his brother close, Lukan's bare back against his chest. He lit two clove cigarettes and gave one of them to Lukan. "Fuck no. Daniel, you're going to have give us a lot more information than that. Like, what the *fuck*, man? We can make this promise to you but we first need to know why other than just that you say so. You don't own us." Kaper withdrew his arms from around his brother and circled around the room, putting Daniel in between the boys. "And *never* handle my brother like that again."

Daniel backed away from them as far as he could, back against the refrigerator, resumed his bottle of wine, emptied it and opened another. Eventually he spoke: "I'm really sorry, you guys. And I do owe you more of an explanation." He took a slow and deep breath. "So, I'm still processing what I saw in there..." and he stopped, fumbled for a cigarette, lit it. The boys watched him, and their eyes seemed to him like dark liquid spirals. "But it can*not* be what anyone else saw. It just *can't*. I could hear the Mayor laughing like a stupid fool at each mirror. But none of what I saw was in the least bit funny." *How much to tell them now?* Daniel wondered. Should he tell them about being visited at his seat by the acrobat Dathan and the human form of the panther Nox? About how he found himself with a cat-stamped pass into that fucked up mirror corridor? Should he tell them about his dream-fogged memory running through the woods naked in a fugue this morning, stalked by that same panther? "I don't want to get into the details right now. I'm *so* tired. But I think that there is something... *evil* in there and I don't want you two exposed to it. It's *wrong*. Dangerous. I don't want you to get hurt. I couldn't stand it." What he didn't tell them—because he'd realized it just then—is that the mirrors were situated directly above the boys' entrance into the crypt. He shuddered at the recollection of that strange sense of an invisible presence in that crypt the last time they'd been down in it.

Daniel tried to pretend that he didn't see the boys have a brief conversation in their weird hand-sign language which ended with the brothers nodding at one another and turning toward Daniel. Said Lukan, "We will do as you say, Daniel."

Daniel thanked them for listening and they stood there quietly smoking their cigarettes for a couple minutes. Eventually Kaper said, "So you guys wanna fuck, or what?"

Daniel let himself be drawn to his bed, let four hands tug away all his clothing and push him into a nest of duvet and pillows, let them do whatever they wanted with his body, did whatever they wanted him to do with theirs.

He awoke just before sunrise, the blue-grey pre-dawn barely lighting his big open bedroom window, sleeping lads to either side of him. He found himself marveling at their simple beauty and how perfect they were for him. Together they were the most incredible sex partners he'd ever had—and he'd had hundreds of them from his training in the capital as a high-end sex worker to his work here after Elspeth had taken the grant money and moved them to Diaspar. They understood every way to touch him, every possible way to use his body for their pleasure and his, every way to bring him to screaming climaxes and to make him do the same for them. Lying there like this between the brothers felt so correct and normal, so much like how life ought to be that he wondered if the entire experience at the circus the night before had really just been a dream. But he knew that he couldn't push it aside like that for very long. He decided he'd spend the day on some research.

T he Mayor is alerted to a disturbing
development.

QUODE APPROACHED the entranced to the infirmary gripped
with dread at what he might see in there. A few minutes
earlier, he'd received a call from Constable Snell asking him
to come over there as soon as possible. "We have a lot of
dead kids this morning, Mister Mayor."

"The plague," Quode had assumed, not wondering in
the moment why this would somehow require notification
from Snell.

"No, sir. This is something else entirely. Doctor Jasper is
away, and her assistant feels that you need to, um, *witness*
in, um, an *official* capacity what we seem to be seeing here."

A miasma of death hung in the air in the vestibule
outside the surgery room. Quode proceeded inward and
was stunned at the site of nine sheet-covered bodies.
Doctor Micah's voice was somewhat shaky as he said, "The

victims are all minors, ranging in age from five to sixteen. The causes of death are various, but none of them died from the current epidemic disease nor even exhibited any signs of infection with it."

Micah drew Quode's attention to a table with two small bodies on it, their skin cold and blue. "Tella, age five and her brother Koman, age seven, children of Rand and Dertha Moralson. Cause of death: drowning." The doctor drew the sheet back over the children's bodies and moved to the next table. "This is Mason Onsuu, age sixteen, son of Morsa Onsuu, single mother. Carbon monoxide asphyxiation appears to be his cause of death."

Doctor Micah looked at Quode's pallor with a twinge of concern. "Are you all right, sir? Do we need to take a break?" Quode shook his head and bade Micah to continue. The doctor drew down the sheets from another pair of siblings. "These boys are Eden and Tor Dastian, ages eight and eleven. They both have very bad fracture injuries to the backs of their skulls. My opinion is that blunt-force trauma to the brain caused their deaths."

Quode, eyebrows raised, looked hard at Micah and then at Snell. "But that sounds like...like they were *killed*. On purpose. Murdered!"

"Sir," said Snell, "our view is that *all* of these children were murdered."

Quode felt briefly dizzy, as if the floor wobbled and spun beneath his feet. Four more bodies lay covered. Micah, a relentless cataloguer of death, showed them to the mayor.

Two more sibling pairs lay dead. Sara and Kendra Bex, ages six and eight, bore obvious ligature marks around their necks indicating strangulation. "And these two," Micah said, presenting Jonny and Argos Vendarm, ages twelve and fourteen, "have been fully exsanguinated."

"What does that mean?" Quode wondered, not really wanting to know.

Micah and Snell exchanged a tense glance. Said Micah, "All the blood has been drained from their bodies." He beckoned Quode to look more closely at the corpses and pointed to large puncture wounds in the boys' throats, under their arms and in their groins.

Snell cleared his throat and said, "Mister Mayor, I will be spending much of the day interviewing the parents of these children. So far, they have all acted shocked, as if they have no idea how any of this could have happened but..."

Quode: "But what?"

"But that doesn't feel credible." Snell cleared his throat and said, "Sir, there's not been a child-murder in this town in a very long time. In about thirty years."

Quode bit back against a surge of nausea and said, "I need the two of you to act with the greatest discretion. Keep all details of this as secret as possible for now. Most particularly the details of what happened to the Vendarm boys." Snell and Micah seemed to look at him blankly as if not understanding his particular emphasis on that case. "The draining of the blood will feed into a narrative that I wish to discourage. Thom Destrin, every night in his pub, is telling people that Mircalla's curse is what brought the plague, and he is gaining adherents. But the curse was specifically that all the children of this town are to die in order to bring a *vampire*—Mircalla—back to life. You see what I mean?"

Micah nodded and Snell said "Of course, sir," and Quode fled the infirmary, thoughts roiled with horror.

CHAPTER

TWELVE

D aniel visits the library and does microfiche
research into the events of thirty years ago.

THE SCENT of old paper and bookbinding glue had a sort of
instant soothing effect on Daniel. He hadn't been to the
library for a few weeks and at once felt like he could spend
the rest of the day there. He descended the tight iron spiral
staircase into the main reading room. He was about to
wonder if anyone else was there when he heard someone
from somewhere behind him say "Hey, faggot!" and laugh
sharply.

Chadon Lyndron, the long-time "acting librarian,"
dashed around from behind his counter and clasped Daniel
in a tight hug. Laughing, Daniel raised the slight man from
the floor briefly, pecked a kiss on his forehead and set him
down. Chadon said, "I'd wondered if you still liked me."

Chadon, a man about a dozen years Daniel's senior but
still very youthful in look and demeanor, had been an occa-

sional sex partner, and an interesting one in that Chadon was, at least as far as Daniel knew, the only transgender guy in this town. And that fact was so completely unapparent to Daniel when they first hooked up that Chadon had needed to explain it. "Before we go much further with this," he'd said, "there's something I'm gonna need you to know." In no way did this information change Daniel's desire to fuck him and they'd proceeded into the first of several encounters.

Chadon dashed back around behind his counter, reached for something beneath it, brought up a trade paperback, gently laid it upon the age-smoothed wood. "Did you come here for this? Did you even know it was out already?"

Daniel picked up the book, its title embossed in gold: *Salò, or the Castrato's Tale.* It was the new novel from Devon Kooper, an American horror writer that Daniel admired. The cover illustration was a somewhat abstract and blurred painting of what might have been young naked men in various states of duress and torture. An eye peered through a die-cut hole in the book's cover. Daniel opened it to see the terrified face of the author himself rendered in a lurid style. "You've read it?"

Chadon nodded. "It scared the fuck out of me. It's really hardcore. Take it with you but promise to bring it back after you're done. I still haven't checked it into the catalog." The librarian seemed to notice the pensiveness in Daniel. He wondered, "Are you looking for something in particular today?"

"This town used to have a newspaper, didn't it?"

"Yeah, up until just a few years ago actually. The *Diaspar Daily Lens and Gleaner.*" Chadon waited for Daniel's expected expression of dismay and disbelief over the name of the paper and, once received, said, "Yes. It's a dumb name, yet it adhered for a century."

"Do you have old issues on microfiche?"

"Of course I do."

"How far back do they go?"

"About a hundred years, since the start of the paper."

"Show me."

Chadon led Daniel into another room with a few ancient study carrels, two of which had microfiche readers. "I'll get some issues for you. Any particular years?"

"Thirty years ago."

"Can you be a little more specific? Like thirty years ago today, or..."

Daniel sighed, unaccountably uncomfortable with making his request so specific. "I want to see what, if anything, was written about the Baron Mircalla being killed by townspeople and his house being burned down. And maybe if there was any reporting on particular events leading up to it."

"There was in fact some such." Chadon frowned slightly. "About a year before that, there was the case of the so-called 'Vampire of Diaspar,' a series of murders over several months that had these things in common: a young victim in his or her teens or twenties; the victim had been missing for a week or more; the victim was eventually found in the Spathe Woods, their body drained of blood and their skin looking like some kind of waxwork. And one other thing that they all had in common: every victim was said to have somehow befriended the Baron and was last seen on their way to the keep. The panic around this was so great that it forced the provincial magistrate to bring the Baron in for questioning."

Daniel, eyes wide: "They arrested *Mircalla*?"

"He offered his cooperation with the investigation. He even went to Transovakia to answer questions before the magistrate. He even let officers of the imperial constabulary conduct a search of the keep."

"And I assume they came up with nothing."

"Nothing. And a few months later, the murders resumed. You can read about it yourself. I'll be right back."

About an hour later, after perusing the scant reporting on the killings and the possible connection to Mircalla, opaqued by the weird diction used by Svardians and Rurimanians in journalism even as recently as three decades ago ("For the Baron, noted of fine blood and bearing, granted the legal authorities the privilege of his time, and with no resulting tarnish upon his dignity, nor even hint of any such, as lord of..." et cetera, on and on like that), Daniel landed on this very brief article...

"The Diaspar Keep, ancestral home of the Baron Mircalla, was razed by fire last night. Given the rapid nature of the fire, as reported by witnesses nearby, and the complete incineration of the structure, it is assumed that the Baron Mircalla died in his house. It is unknown if the Baron has any heirs who might succeed him in his appointment to this barony." This tiny report was accompanied by a photo of Mircalla, taken months earlier as he was leaving the courthouse in Transovakia.

And that was all. Nothing about the run-up to the fire, nothing about townspeople invading the property and confronting Mircalla. And not a word about the two final murders that some people had attributed to Mircalla: the girl Juyann and her brother Jahn, children of then-schoolmaster Damon Stukas. If he'd pressed on through a few more months of newspapers, Daniel may have spotted a brief obituary for the schoolmaster stating that he'd died in his sleep of an unknown cause, and that he'd been pre-deceased by his wife and his two children. And nothing at all about him spending much of his final months on Earth trying to get other key figures in the town to admit to what they'd done together and what they'd all seen that night. No one wanted to talk about it anymore. They'd over-thrown their lord and had apparently done this without any repercussion, and they wanted no more of it. Surely no one wanted to humor Stukas's constant attempts to get people to acknowledge that his children had been seduced, raped and vampirised by the dead Baron.

Daniel stared at the picture of the Baron, trying to imagine this photo as a real document of an actual super-natural monster. He felt Chadon return and lean in toward the screen.

Chadon leaned in still closer, peered at the black and white image of the Baron, his tousled dark hair and bright silver nitrate eyes, his muscular arms exposed to the shoul-ders by his sleeveless tunic, and again, those eyes. "This is really weird," he said. "I've seen these pictures of him before, but..."

"But what?"

"I've never noticed this before, Daniel...but you look just like him."

Daniel stared more closely at the image and started to see what Chadon saw: the hair, the shape of the face, the nose, the chin, those eyes. As he stared, he thought he saw the old picture move just slightly, like frames of a film passing very slowly through a projector, the smallest turn of Mircalla's head toward Daniel. And the corners of the Baron's mouth rose just a little bit, sketching the coldest smile ever.

CHAPTER

THIRTEEN

Quode encounters Magran and Kasyn at the bakery; they discuss a trade and Quode is invited to the second performance of the Circus of Nights.

ON THE WAY back to his office, Quode observed the circus leaders—Magran, the mistress of ceremonies and the panther-tamer Kasyn—exit Rue Morgellen's bakery, the bell on the door jangling, Rue following them out saying "Here! I almost forgot!" and handing a box of something, perhaps some donuts or croissants, to Magran. "And thanks again!"

The circus duo crossed the street at an angle, roughly in Quode's direction, saw him, waved, and Magran said, "Good morning, Mister Mayor! How are you today?"

Before he could even answer, she was standing before him, opening her bakery box. "Would you care for one of these orange-cardamom sticky buns?"

Quode chuckled nervously and demurred with, "Ah,

thank you, no. I'm trying to cut back on the sweets, you see. But Miss Rue's pastries *are* top quality."

Kasyn smiled and said, "I'm sure our crew will devour them happily. They are a sweet token of thanks for a happy trade that we were able to make with Miss Rue."

"A trade?" Quode didn't know why exactly, but he found it vaguely off-putting that the circus people were conducting any sort of commerce in the town. And Kasyn uneased him with a distinct aura of erotic depravity, much like that which clung to Daniel Jasper except even more outlandish in its expression.

"Yes," said Kasyn. "The cordon that has cut off your town has blocked some of her supplies from getting in. She said that she is running perilously low on white flour. Our chef, however, has loads of it. And when he heard that Miss Rue had on hand a lot of the very fine pomegranate molasses that's to be found in these parts, he proposed a trade." He leaned in and lowered his voice as if sharing the most confidential of information. "The pomegranate molasses, you see, is an ingredient in the shawarma that he makes for our concession stand."

Quode gave this information an exaggerated nod of comprehension. "Oh, I see. Yes, of course. Well, how fortuitous for everyone then."

"So, Mister Mayor," Magran said, "I certainly noticed you in the front row at our performance last night. Did you find it enjoyable or at least interesting?"

Quode exerted himself to smile. He really wanted to get back to his office. "Oh yes, indeed! Really quite remarkable. I've certainly never seen anything quite like it. And I am sure it's the talk of the town today, with everyone speculating on how you achieved some of your illusions."

Kasyn said, holding his unblinking gaze upon Quode,

"It's always interesting to see which things people assume are *illusions* versus what really happened."

Magran reached toward Quode and tucked a slip of paper into his front shirt pocket. "Be our guest again tonight. We vary the program from one night to the next so that it can be enjoyed more than once without being too repetitious."

"Ah, well," Quode nodded. "Thank you. If I can make it, I will look forward to seeing your performance again."

Magran and Kasyn, in synch, performed a little bow to the Mayor, smiled and turned away and walked serenely down the sidewalk and toward their encampment. Quode watched them until they disappeared around a corner and he could not shake off an inexplicable sensation of danger around that pair. Or was it just nervousness emanating from the fact that they were something new in a town where a new thing happened so infrequently? *Many new things lately,* he thought. The disease and its fatalities. The arrival of the Circus of Nights. The ghastly murders of children. *Are they all connected? Could Destrin be right?* The thought sickened him.

CHAPTER
FOURTEEN

Daniel, seeking supernatural insight into what may be happening to him, visits an old friend; a session of automatic writing and a terrifying revelation.

"JUST COME RIGHT ON IN!" hailed a familiar voice, as if suspended in the air above him, as Daniel trod the cobbled pathway to Rhoda Chordisaul's front door. He hadn't even called ahead to announce his visit. Was she watching through her front window? It would not have surprised Daniel in the least if Rhoda had just somehow known all day that he was about to arrive with a question, a request— known it even before he himself had thought of it.

The weathered and paint-stripped front door swung inward as if of its own power and Daniel stepped into the front parlor. He noted that it was now even more choked with bric-a-brac and dusty clutter than it had been during his last visit just a couple weeks ago. He gasped and backed away from something that he'd not yet even seen consciously: a life-size mannequin of a teenage boy leered at him. Its cricket uniform looked to be brand new, an athletic supporter on the outside of the pants, black smudges beneath its shiny blue rollerball eyes, a cap askew on the crown of its blond-doll-haired head. "What are *you* looking at?" Daniel muttered, stepping past the mannequin. The eyes seemed to follow him. Did the head turn slightly? He paused, gave the thing a hard glare. He called out loudly: "Where are you, Rhoda?"

"In the meditation room, kiddo!" The old woman's voice seemed to emanate from within the walls.

Daniel stepped carefully through the front parlor and then the dining room and then the kitchen and, eventually, he reached the so-called meditation room which was, in fact, an enclosed back porch festooned with purple silk curtains and with candelabra and talking boards and tarot decks and crystal balls sitting on every available surface. Rhoda sat at her small table in the room's center, cloaked in a gold and green paisley dress, a black feather boa draped over her shoulders. She grinned broadly at Daniel. A beam of sunset peering through the drapes set her crown of dyed red hair alight. "Daniel, my sweetness! How nice of you to visit your lonely old Auntie Rhoda this afternoon!" She rose from her seat and rushed up against Daniel, giving him a soft but all-encompassing embrace. She broke the hug and looked up at his eyes, stroked his one-day chin-scruff with two fingers. "I swear, Daniel, you've grown two inches since I last saw you!"

"Rhoda, as I've told you many times, I've stood at this height since before you ever met me." He pecked at her cheek and added, "But perhaps *you* have shrunk a bit in your ever-older age!"

Rhoda applied a light slap to Daniel's left cheek and

chortled, the voice of her laugh like the clattering of seashell wind chimes. "You're a very sassy boy, as always, my Daniel." She stepped over to a sidebar and fussed about with crystal rocks glasses and a black bottle. "It is about *that* time of the afternoon," she said, "and I'll offer you some absinthe if you're not here just to tease and berate a helpless old lady."

Daniel smiled and found himself, unaccountably, brushing away from his eyes a few tears. "I'm happy to enjoy a drink with you, Auntie, and I pray that such will lubricate our conversation because I do have a special request to make of you."

Rhoda strained the liqueur through sugar cubes and handed a glass to Daniel. "A toast," she said, raising her glass, "to my most *favorite* nephew."

Daniel gulped the shot and handed the glass back to Rhoda for a refill and let her know that she need not bother with the sugar. "You've yet to tell me who any of your *other* nephews are so that I might know to whom I'm being compared."

Rhoda squinted at him. "You know they're all long dead, my sweet, and buried under my house!"

"I wouldn't doubt it!" Daniel seated himself at Rhoda's table. "May I?" He pointed at an open velvet-black box of Rurimanian cigarettes. Rhoda took two, lit them both between her lips and handed him one.

"Oh, your cute friends Kaper and Lukan were here again just the other day."

Daniel: "Hopefully they weren't too annoying. I sometimes wonder if I ever should have introduced them to you."

"Nonsense! They are perfect dolls. Kaper wants to learn the tarot, so I have been giving him instruction. I can tell that Lukan thinks it's all bullshit but he's not rude to his brother about it. When he gets bored, he wanders off and does useful things around the house."

Daniel nearly spat his drink. "*Lukan* does useful things around the house! Like what?"

"Well, for your information," said Rhoda with great gravity, "he repaired the broken Babylonian tiles in the bathroom and did quite a fine job of it."

"Unbelievable. I won't let him know that you revealed to me the secret that he has useful skills."

They sat and sipped their drinks and smoked for a bit, saying nothing.

Daniel knew it was his turn to ask his question, but he stalled. Rhoda replaced their absinthe glasses with wine glasses and poured two huge servings of icy sauvignon blanc. "All right, come out with it, boy," she said. "I have sensed all day that you would show up needing something. So don't be shy now."

Daniel pressed his palms to his eyes and sighed. "I want to ask you to try to...*write* something for me."

"*Write* something, you say?"

"Yes, Auntie Rhoda."

She seemed to churn a bit in her chair before she said, "And you are sure that *writing* is the course to your answer and that we can't find it by, oh, something easy like a session on the talking board or a long hard look into your pretty brown eyes?"

Daniel stood, exited the room, and returned a moment later with a stack of parchment paper from Rhoda's kitchen. "No. Neither of those methods will work for this. I'm certain."

Rhoda arranged the paper in a neat stack upon the tabletop and pointed at a bureau drawer, telling Daniel wordlessly to fetch the markers from it. He set an assortment of the thick pens at her hands. Said she, "And do you have a certain subject in mind? Something in particular that you think I may be inclined to write about?"

Daniel sighed, bowed his head, so signaled his sudden rawness. He did not speak of the strange sense of presence in the crypt, of the panther and the fugue in the woods, of his bizarre burst of violence on Lukan, but he finally said, "I think it might be about me. I must admit I'm a bit scared. I think there's something very *wrong* with me."

Rhoda nodded very slightly, very slowly. "You may be right about that. You have good instincts." She leaned back in her chair and smiled. "You know, I assume, that I'll want you to sing for me. So that we may set the correct mood."

Daniel groaned. "Is that *really* necessary? It always makes me feel so foolish."

"You'll humor me, kiddo, and my arcane ways." She pointed at the little harpsichord against the far wall. "It will go more easily for us if you play and sing our song. And you *know* that."

"All right. Fine." Daniel sighed and seated himself upon the bench before the harpsichord. "So, are you ready?"

Rhoda frowned slightly, and she seemed to look *past* Daniel, as if at something beyond him. "Just play, and then we'll see...together."

Daniel fingered the keys, coaxing the music from the badly tuned instrument, and he sang:

Cherry-ripe, ripe, ripe, I cry
Full and fair ones; come and buy
If so be you ask me where
They do grow, I answer: There
Where my Julia's lips do smile;
There's the land, or cherry-isle

Whose plantations fully show
All the year where cherries grow

Daniel commenced repeating the short song and felt his spine thrill with a chill when he heard Rhoda say in a voice not quite her own, "Yes. I see it. *Yes!* A force of horror. Wicked this way it comes." She wrote upon the pages, two-handed, throwing one to the side and starting upon the next. Said she, "Daniel at a doorway. A *thing* upon him. A thing setting upon him, wrapping him with arms and claws...Yes. Yes." Sharply she said. "Back away, boy."

Daniel quit playing the song and approached the table where Rhoda was already filling a third page with her sprawling and baroque antique scrawl. "Back away from what, Rhoda?" he whispered.

He pulled away the nearly finished third page and she put her marker to the next. He'd learned from past experiences with this technique to try to keep the pages in sequence rather than let them fall to the floor in disorder.

"That door, kid," she said, still writing. "It opens into you, and *you* open into *it.*" More scrawling, more hurriedly now. "Doors and mirrors—mirrors can be portals." Rhoda gasped. *"Names.* I see them: Dathan...Chlora...*twins*...twins of evil. They change shape, like liquid. They can go anywhere."

"But who are they really, Rhoda? What are they doing here? What's their purpose?"

"The Circus of Nights," said Rhoda, looking up at Daniel clear-eyed almost as if the trance were broken, but her eyes glazed and rolled back again. "You go through that door and...and...more names: Kasyn...and *Magran,* but *she* was once known by another name. *Here!* Thirty years ago. She has returned. She prays in a crypt of night-moss."

Daniel pulled away the next sheet and Rhoda continued

writing. He could make out the name Kasyn several times. He asked, "*Who* is Kasyn in all this? What's his role?"

"A dark magic force. A thing of horror—supremely powerful." She gasped again and said, "Kin of Mircalla."

Daniel shuddered, deeply chilled. He watched that name form on Rhoda's page: *Mircalla*. "Are you seeing the Circus of Nights and Kasyn as having something to do with Mircalla...now, in the present day?" *Is this even possible?* he thought. *That I could be in the middle of something like this?*

Rhoda's scrawling sped up. "I see puzzle pieces...no! Game pieces on a warped board." She begins drawing geometric symbols, characters that look to Daniel like zodiac signs and ancient numerals. "Mircalla moves the pieces from behind the veil of death. Kasyn is his set of hands in the physical plane." She filled another page and then another with more of the bizarre symbology. "He's going to open a door into Hell."

"The Circus of Nights is the door, Daniel." Rhoda's hand slowed, spasmed a bit, and then the ink stopped flowing. "Close it. And walk away." Rhoda set down the marker and reclined a bit in her chair. She pointed to her wine glass and Daniel handed it to her. She drank it one long pull and said, "Well. *That* was fun."

Daniel rolled the sheets of parchment and set them on the table. "May I keep these?"

"Of course."

"Do you remember what you saw? Can you talk about it at all? The key seems to be that circus that's in town now, and the figure that you identified as Kasyn—he's real, I've seen him—and a connection somehow to the legend of Mircalla."

Rhoda pointed at her empty glass. Daniel refilled it. She said, "I know you won't listen to me, but if you were half as smart as you think you are, you'd stay the hell away from that circus and those people. Didn't you tell me once that you have family in French Guiana?"

"In the Dutch Argentine actually," Daniel said.

"Right now would be a great time for you to go abroad for a few weeks, but I know you won't." Rhoda sighed and said, "These circus people...they think they are here at Mircalla's command. I can't see the details of their plan, but the only reason they came to this town is *because* Mircalla somehow exerted such dark power from beyond his grave. But even *they* don't know exactly how their plan will work out."

Daniel started to speak, stopped, reframed his question and resumed. "Then why this whole elaborate circus production? It's so over the top. And why am I not sure that I even *want* to know?"

Rhoda gazed at Daniel, a great sadness seeming to well in her eyes. "I must tell you something now. You're carrying a shadow with you, Daniel, a black cloak with arms like broken wings, a wraith-thing, that wants to reach around you." She heaved a stuttering sigh and continued: "I saw it precede you into the room. Its arms led your way up the path to my door. I've told you before that the color of your aura is a pinkish purple, shot through with lightning, like the way that they talk about the other-light in the colour-out-of-space zones, and it still is that color. But it's being clouded, dimmed by this shadow that you drag with you like an anchor, that tries to cloak you and pull you down completely."

Daniel inhaled deeply and felt, literally, his heart thump inside his chest. He said, "Are you saying that they are here for *me?*"

"I'm saying that *you* might be in *their* way."

"What does this...this shadow, this *cloak* look like? How big is it?"

Rhoda took a sip of wine and sighed. "At certain moments it's bigger than this house, Daniel. I can see it swell through the walls sometimes to thrice the size it was when you arrived. And I think what we just did now may somehow have fed it." She rose from her chair, grabbed up the pages from her automatic writing, thrust them into Daniel's hands. "I love you, kid. But I need you to take this *thing* away from here *now*. I can't bear it!"

Daniel, his eyes burst full of tears, half-blinded, obeyed the old woman and fled the house, pausing for a moment at the front door, half-blocked by the mannequin in the cricket uniform. Its head spun around and around and around and it seemed to say and say and say the nonsense word *"sussurus"* again and again and again. Daniel, breathless in his horror, elbowed past the thing and ran and ran and ran.

CHAPTER

FIFTEEN

L ater that evening, Daniel sneaks down into the crypt while the circus performs above him.

IT WASN'T ANYWHERE NEAR as difficult sneaking into the hall of mirrors and finding the hidden crypt entrance as Daniel had feared. He entered the circus as a last-minute guest, bought a ticket and carefully worked his way out of sight behind the tent that housed the mirrors, which was standing unattended at that point since it wouldn't be in business until after the show. In the dark, roughly behind where the fifth and sixth mirrors stood, he found parked one of their vehicles and beneath it the thatch-covered wood panel that could be slid aside to expose the crumbling steps into the underground chamber. He crawled under the steam van, found the hidden trap door, opened it, dropped inside and pulled the panel closed over himself in total darkness before lighting his galvanic lucifer and starting the descent into the necropolis.

Kaper and Lukan were attending that night's perfor-mance, and he'd told them they could come to his house afterward and spend the night but to expect him to be very late getting back home. He'd told him that he was going to spend some of the evening with Rhoda, possibly have drinks later with Chadon at the library and then see if he could get some business among the circus crew after the show. If successful, he'd said, this might keep him busy until dawn. He was unhappy with himself for lying to them. And he hoped they'd keep their promise to him not to go through the Mirrors of Truths and Lies after the show. If they would just avoid that, he thought, they'd be safe from whatever was happening to him.

CHAPTER
SIXTEEN

A few hours later at Daniel's house, Kaper and Lukan are visited by the circus acrobats.

LUKAN, in that liminal state between dream-sleep and awareness, pulled Kaper closer, spooning him, resting his chin in his sweat-brother's hair. His penis stiffened against the small of Kaper's back, and Kaper made a small sound and seemed to say something like, *I can hear them, too*, but Lukan wasn't sure if he'd understood that correctly or if he'd heard his brother speak at all. But then he heard another voice cross the horizon of dreaming: *They're pretty, aren't they? I love it that they're twins like us.* And another voice, more feminine: *And apparently lovers like us.* A pause, and *That one is almost awake. He can hear us in his head. You take him, brother. I'll awaken the sleeper.*

Lukan felt it before he could see it, a body—hot fevered skin—the weight of another person in bed with them. He let himself be pulled away from Kaper and onto his back by hot hands, and then he saw Dathan, that circus boy who could fly like bats, his skin a canvas of indecipherable drawings, lower his mouth to Lukan's. He felt a dull pressure and a slight pain and tasted metal in his mouth. *He bit my lip!* Unable to react, so sluggish was his brain and body, he let Dathan force his tongue into his mouth, and to draw blood a second time. The circus creature raised his mouth from Lukan's and smiled down at the boy. He let a streamer of bloody spit fall from his mouth into Lukan's. The boy gaped, mouth like a nestling, asked for more, sucked in Dathan's tongue again. He heard Kaper whimper beside him and ask what's happening, voice still sleep-sodden. Dathan let him turn to his left and he saw the girl version of Dathan—Chlora was her name—lift her face from Kaper's chest, her chin and lips smeared bright red. She lowered her head again and lapped more blood from the wound she'd opened around the boy's left nipple. *I should be screaming. She's hurting him.* But he could not catch the breath for it nor even gather the fear. Dathan punctured Lukan's bottom lip once more with a fang, and this time it didn't even hurt. That voice in his head again: *I don't want you to be scared. I don't want this to hurt.* Lukan hadn't even realized that this cock was stiff until he felt it slide into the hot clenching sheath of Dathan's ass. It was tighter than Kaper's or Daniel's and so much warmer. He looked to his left and saw his brother, chest and belly smeared with his blood, instinctively thrust his hips upward into Chlora. She smiled down at him and pressed her hand to chest and kneaded more blood from his body between her fingers. Dathan, to his sister: "Careful. If he puts his nut in you, you'll end up pregnant."

Chlora smiled. "Imagine how beautiful the child will be. We'll raise him together. We'll make him one of us."

"I'll make *him* one of us!" Dathan, bent forward, still riding Lukan's cock, and sucked blood from the boy's lips again. He glanced at Chlora. She nodded.

Dathan's left index finger seemed now to end in a steel claw. Lukan watched curiously, that claw as it lowered to his chin. And then Dathan pulled that claw down making a red weeping wound from Lukan's throat down to his navel and said into the boy's head, *"I'm going to kill your body so that you can live again—with me—and forever!"*

Lukan tried to be afraid but couldn't. He fucked hard into Dathan's cunt. He reached up for Dathan's neck and gripped the circus boy's ornate leather choker that trapped within it weave a lot of shining beads and rings of osmium. Dathan let the boy pull his head closer by the necklace. Lukan said, "It's going to hurt, isn't it?" Next to him, he thought he could hear Kaper scream, but the sound was muffled by the warm pulse of Dathan's thoughts in his head. *Yes. It will. But not for very long at all and, afterward, you'll never feel pain again.*

Dathan opened his mouth beneath Lukan's right ear and clenched his fangs hard against the boy's throat and opened a gushing well of blood. Lukan shuddered into orgasm, spurted thick streams of semen into Dathan's gut. Dathan gulped from the boy's spurting throat. He spat some of it over Lukan's face and into his mouth and went back down, opening the tear wider, sucking harder on the boy's life-force. He glanced over to Kaper and saw Chlora virtually bathing in the ruin she'd made of her boy from his throat to his pelvis. Kaper, eyes seeming to dim, met Lukan's gaze and seemed to say, See *you on the other side, brother.*

Side by side the brothers' clocks stopped, fucked to death by the circus twins. But death didn't seem to take away awareness. It was still the dream-liminal state, but sharper, brighter, as if seeing with new colors. "You must drink, before it's too late. The power spoils quickly." That was Chlora, still hovering over Kaper. Lukan saw her claw a deep wound into her left breast, nearly severing the nipple and she pressed the gushing wound to Kaper's open mouth. "You must drink, and then you'll come back to life."

"Same for you, stud," said Dathan. Smiling down at Lukan, he told the boy to watch and do what he's told. Dathan grabbed the head of his stiff cock with one hand, and with the other, drew the claw down its underside, opening a gash from his piss-slit to his ballsack. He arched forward, crotch over Lukan's face. "Open." Lukan opened. "Suck, boy." Lukan swallowed the bleeding cock all the way, past his tonsils and somehow managed not to gag or choke. Dathan pressed his hands hard against the boy's ears and fucked down harder into his throat. After a dozen or two more thrusts, he pulled his cock from Lukan's mouth and stroked the bloody member with one hand, aiming the head at Lukan's eyes. The lad was blinded briefly by jets of Dathan's scalding semen. Dathan laughed, lowered his mouth to the boy's face and licked the cum from his eyelids. "You'll rest now. For just a little while as your bodies heal from what we did to them. The change is happening fast. We'll clean up the place a bit before we go. Maybe flip this mattress and put on a new sheet. You'll hardly feel us moving you around. You may be able to hear us talk, but it will seem like a dream."

Lukan could still hear them, faintly, voices like echoes in a cave. "Fucking hell, Dathan," the girl said. "So dramatic a choice. Of course you heal quickly, but didn't that hurt like mad?"

Said Dathan, "A bit. But I don't get to turn a boy like

that one very often, so I figured I'd treat myself to the most mind-blowing fucking blowjob ever." Lukan felt his cock stiffen again. He wanted to reach for it, maybe start jerking off in front of Dathan to let him know that he wanted more sex, that he wanted to fuck the circus boy's ass again, but he was too inert with drowsiness. He heard this: "Did he put his cum in you?" Chlora: "Of course. We'll see if anything happens with that."

Dathan said something like, "Kasyn's going to be fucking furious with us. We were supposed to have killed them in the crypt and given all their blood to Mircalla but, of course—us being us!—we turned them instead and let one of them knock you up," and Chlora said something about how they were just too pretty to waste and how they'll be more valuable as members of the troupe or something like that—he really wasn't sure he understood what they're saying at all, it was all so weird, it was all so fucked —and then Lukan faded out entirely, tipping over and sinking into deep sleep's vast chasm.

CHAPTER
SEVENTEEN

Daniel attempts a communion in the crypt; a visitation by Kasyn; an erotic nightmare under the spell of a vampire.

IN THE TOMB CHAMBER, Daniel unpacked a little box of votive candles that he and the boys had stowed there and set them around, some on the altar, some on Mircalla's sarcophagus. He centered the spirit board on the altar and centered the green glass planchette on it. He lit three sticks of nagchampa and said, "If anyone is here tonight, know that my mind and heart are open and that I seek communication. Know that I am not afraid and that you cannot harm me." From beneath the altar, he brought up a silver chalice like they'd use for wine in the church and into it he poured a little bit of Chartreuse from a dusty bottle. With a straight razor, he sliced a short gash into the palm of his left hand and let the blood drip into the chalice and mix with the green liquor. "I seek the opening of the mind and the body, the body and the blood." And he drank from the chalice and said, "Can anyone hear me?"

The planchette slid to YES. Chilled to the bone, Daniel smiled, thrilled. It had never moved before without him touching it. "Who is here with me?"

The glass slid across the board and spelled a name: KASYN. He was not exactly surprised by this information, but he was not expecting such a straightforward answer. "Are you saying that you can hear me?"

YES, said the board.

Daniel glanced around in candlelit gloom. "But *how* can you hear me? In what way are you here?"

The planchette slid over letters and Daniel followed it carefully as it spelled out...B-E-H-I-N-D-Y-O-U.

Daniel gasped and had just barely started to turn around when he felt himself embraced, lifted from the floor, pulled into the arms of the circus master who pressed his lips to Daniel's and nicked his lower lip with a fang. Daniel tried to pull away but Kasyn easily held him in place and again pressed his mouth to Daniel's and made it bleed. And then after another moment or two of this, Kasyn released him, set his feet back to the floor and said, "Are you always so open to the mouth of a strange man? Do your cute twin boyfriends mind?"

Daniel wanted to ask how the hell Kasyn knows about them but then realized that, of course he would know, and so he said instead, "I'm a sex worker. I've had sex with hundreds of men. They are aware of it."

Kasyn tugged open Daniel's pants and gripped his stiffening penis. "That's good. I figured they are probably as sweetly slutty as you anyway after I saw them down here with you. At first, I thought you'd be just a trio of dumb goth boys playing with a spirit board, but I could tell right away that you are a lot more than that." Daniel shuddered at a recollection that he could not quite pull all the way back into clear memory. "Yeah, that was me," Kasyn said. "That weird feeling you had that someone was down here with you and your pretty cocksuckers. You were right. I was right here with you, but you couldn't see or hear me because of a trick I played on your mind, a trick a lot like one I want to try on you now while I fuck you."

Daniel tried to recoil from Kasyn, but the vampire held him too tightly. Daniel said, "I don't want you to play any more tricks on me. You cannot harm me. You have to let me go now."

Kasyn nibbled at Daniel's neck just below his left ear. "I can't let you go now. And I'm not really giving you a choice in what's going to happen to you next so you may as well just lie back and let it flow over you and into you. In a moment, you're going to feel very relaxed, and my voice will sound like it's coming from a dream, like this...

...Daniel, listen to me: I want you to hear me in your body, and hear me as a vessel for everything you've ever wanted. Come down with me into the deep spunk of your dreams. You spill your spunk on the floor and take one step forward into it and you slip and fall, your ass and back flat to the tile. I see the shape of my cousin in you, your body as the body of Mircalla. All you lack is his spirit. I want to fuck it into you. I don't care if it hurts. You saw it didn't you, I know you did but you won't open your mind to mine. You know what's inside my cousin's sarcophagus and you hide this knowledge from me and if you won't share it, then I will fuck it out of you. That will be fun for me, and I'll keep on doing it to you until you give yourself up to me fully. You can't win, Daniel. I've been at this since Commodus ruled the Roman Empire. We're ancient people. You can be too.

Remember a few days ago how you fucked that dirty little

faggot Lukan while his brother watched you and stroked his cock? I know your fantasy, Daniel. The exact thing that flared in your fuck-addled mind, this: impregnate Lukan! Get that young fuck knocked up with your sperm, Daniel. Make him bear your child and then raise the kid to be just like you, a male body made for men to enjoy, a lithe body awash in the spit and piss and semen of hundreds of men. But it's a thing you can't have, but maybe you could get closer to it if you could turn those boys into creatures like us.

Us? Daniel groaned as Kasyn's fever-hot cock seemed to swell even further inside the cavity of his ass. Kasyn raked sharp fingernails from Daniel's navel to his throat, scratching a path of blood. *Your blood will make me spill cum, Daniel. I wish I could drink of it fully. I fucking ache to turn you into one of us now, but I can't. I don't think it would even work if I tried, but I dare not anyway because that is not Mircalla's plan for us, for you.* Daniel winced as Kasyn opened more wounds with his nails, cutting into the soft skin of his armpits, new blood soaking the thick sweat-swamped black hair. The vampire lowered his mouth to each pit, lapped up some of the blood, forced himself to stop, fucked harder into Daniel's ass, making the boy cry out loudly. *You're taking my cum, Daniel!* And Daniel gasped at the heat of it, the sensation like a jet of near-scalding water flooding his hole for a whole minute while Kasyn shuddered and pushed and moaned above him. *It's just a dream Daniel. You're only dreaming but you'll know me better when we meet again in real life.* The presence of Kasyn seemed to grow lighter and fainter and then it evanesced completely, and Daniel fell backward into wakefulness. If this had really been a dream like Kasyn had said then why was Daniel naked, and why did he have bloody scratches down the length of his torso and under his arms and semen leaking from his ass? He dressed and blearily made his way to the crypt's exit just beneath the mirrors. When he reached the outdoors, he saw that it was well past sunrise, nearly noon. He'd been in the crypt all night.

CHAPTER

EIGHTEEN

T he Destrin twins, shiny and new, try out their new bodies.

IT TOOK a little while for the boys to get cleaned up and dressed once they'd finally awakened from the intense slumber of their resurrection. They lay together on a sweat-damp sheet, gazing at each other, marveling at how good they felt, and how good they looked and how hot their newly healed skin was. They embraced first with arms and then with mouths, flooding each other's tongues with spit. They fucked for an hour, continually trading positions, each boy filling the other's hole with cum again and again. Eventually they decided to take a break from this even though their erections would not deflate. They stepped together into Daniel's shower and washed each other's bodies and fell into another brief fuck-session, Lukan pressing his brother against the shower wall, retaking him from behind, dumping another load into his hole. They dried off and stole some clothes from Daniel. They pomaded their hair and put on sunglasses and stepped out into high noon sunlight, shiny and new and glittering.

They were headed—eventually—toward the circus tent (thinking they may see if they can sneak down into the crypt) and choosing the wooded path that opens into the disused so-called Old Cemetery, when they heard voices somewhere far behind them. "Are they calling our names?" Kaper wondered. "Is that really what's happening right now? And, if so, *why* the fuck?"

Lukan, listening with his new ears said. "They're looking for us. And Daniel. They've been to the house. I know that somehow. It's Father Zulemus and Constable Snell. Jesus Christ, I hate those assholes. Fuck the church, fuck the cops."

Kaper said, "Let's play a funny game, brother."

Lukan, grinning: "What do you have in mind, lover?"

Kaper opened his mouth, let his fangs get aroused, let drool drip from their points. He pulled Lukan close and put his dripping wet mouth against Lukan's hot neck. Lukan smiled. "I think I know what you have in mind. That *will* be really funny!"

The searchers drew closer, close enough that their noise on the path was annoyingly loud in the boys' new ears. Kaper licked his brother's throat just under his left ear and took a bite.

CHAPTER
NINETEEN

Quode receives an update on dead and missing children; Snell notes that the Destrin brothers are missing and goes to look for them; Thom Destrin disputes what he is being told about his sons.

MAYOR QUODE LISTENED to the morning's update from Constable Snell and Doctor Micah. "If there's any good news in this," Snell said, "it's that we have *only* two new deaths to report. But we started the morning missing a bunch of kids. Panicked parents reported in starting very early. We have located nearly all of the missing, but we have a weird situation going on now where a lot of them refuse to go home. They say there's something wrong with their parents. They're afraid of them. For the moment, Father Zulemus and Sister Aquaria are accommodating some of them at the church until we can sort this out."

Quode sighed. "And the two deaths? How?"

"Exsanguinated again," said Micah.

"My god, this is horrible." Quode rubbed his eyes. "I'm so tired. I wish I'd not gone to the circus last night. But all the missing kids have been found?"

"The reported ones anyway," Snell said. "I happened to see Thom Destrin in passing a short while ago and he mentioned that he hadn't seen his sons since sometime early yesterday, but he thought they might be staying at Daniel Jasper's house. They're a bit older now, technically adults now, but it might be worth just checking in to see if they're safe. Zulemus said he'd go and check, but I don't want him doing it alone, so I'll run over there with him and be back in a little while."

About a half hour later, Snell called Quode and Micah on the phone from the constabulary office and asked them to come quickly to Destrin's pub. They'd found Kaper and Lukan and they were about to give Thom Destrin some terrible news.

A few minutes later and a couple hours before normal opening time, Thom Destrin, standing behind his long ancient teakwood bar and polishing glasses said, "All right, tell me one more time what you saw and when you saw it, because this is not adding up."

Snell, trying for a tone of great empathy said, "Thom, I know this has to be the worst thing that anyone could ever—"

Destrin raised a hand and shushed the constable. "Just humor me for a moment. Because what you said the first time doesn't add up timewise, you see. So, once more: when did you find the boys, and how long do you think they'd been lying there like that?"

Quode winced at *"like that."* And he really didn't want to hear again the details of how the brothers lay dead with their throats torn open as if by a savage animal. They'd already speculated about the giant panther from the circus. The death van had probably picked up the bodies by now and would have brought them to the infirmary for their father to eventually identify.

Snell checked his wristwatch. "About an hour ago. I'd guess they'd been there perhaps a few hours." He looked hard at Quode and added, "There's no reason to keep this a secret from Thom. My opinion, based on several other cases we've seen, is that the ultimate cause of death was exsanguination."

Destrin shook his head slowly and chuckled. "If they've been dead in that woods for hours, then how do you explain the fact that I saw Lukan not five minutes before you all got here sneaking in and out of my storeroom back there to steal a pack of smokes? I'm sure he thinks I didn't know he was here because those boys think I'm dumb as rocks, but I did not imagine it, Mister Mayor and Mister Constable and Father Zulemus *and* Doctor Micah."

And then a voice from somewhere behind Destrin said, "Father, what is going on in here?" and Kaper and Lukan passed through the swinging kitchen doors into the barroom. Destrin gestured broadly toward them with an open palm as if to say *"Ta-da!* You see?"

Zulemus seemed to blanch. He crossed himself and took a couple steps back, eyes focused on the brothers, mouth agape. He said, "This is not possible." He looked to Snell who looked back at him dumbfounded. "We saw what we saw, Snell." The constable failed to reply. Zulemus withdrew the rosary from under his cloak and began to intone the Lord's Prayer which elicited a roar of derision from Thom Destrin.

"Knock it off with that, Father," said the publican. "Somehow, some way, the two of you were plainly mistaken in what you saw because, as you can clearly see, my sons are standing right here and quite alive."

"My god!" Kaper cried. "Were they telling you that we were *dead?*"

"This is *insane!*" yelled Lukan, and then more quietly to his father, "Dad, I'm sorry about stealing the smokes. I'll ask next time." Destrin smiled and winked at the boy.

Kaper paced the length of the bar, shaking his head, fists clenched. "I can't believe you'd do this to our dad. All this horror and disease and tragedy happening in our town and all of you great and important men of Diaspar somehow have *nothing* better to do than come in here and terrorize our father with this hoax that we've been killed. This is just the worst."

"Unreal," Lukan concurred. "You should all be ashamed of yourselves." And to his father, softly: "I'm glad we showed up when we did, Dad. We'd have hated for you to have worried so."

Micah backed himself toward the door saying he needed to get back to the infirmary followed closely by Quode who muttered to Destrin that he was glad that everything turned out all right after all. Zulemus followed them, never quite taking his eyes off the twins until he, too, was out the door.

Snell lingered for a moment, looking at Destrin and the boys, confused, slowly shaking his head. "I'm sorry about this, Thom. I just...don't know. I can't explain it. We *did* see...something." He focused on Kaper and Lukan. "But I guess it wasn't these guys. Well, thank God for that anyway." The constable waved a weak goodbye and exited the pub.

Destrin laughed and said, "Those dumbasses." He looked at his sons, raised an eyebrow. "You lads are awfully dressed up for the middle of a Thursday afternoon. You have dates for lunch or something?"

Lukan smiled. "We thought we might go see if anyone good is hanging out at Kyban's," and pointed in the general direction of the diner in the town square.

And Kaper added, "We think we'll go to the circus again tonight. It's the last night. We'll probably crash at Daniel's house again, so don't worry if you don't see us again tonight."

Destrin nodded. "Your mum and I might go up to the circus tonight, too. No one will be in here tonight anyway with that going on."

"Terrific!" Lukan said. "We'll look for you!"

Destrin considered his sons with a sudden look of somberness. "Actually, I think it's good that you've been staying close to Daniel Jasper. That boy seems charmed somehow. You're probably safer near him until all this evil business in this town has passed."

The brothers looked at each other, nonplussed by this uncharacteristically concerned statement from their father. They each walked around behind the bar and gave Thom Destrin a hug.

The boys stepped out into the street and into the heat of the afternoon sun and considered which way to walk. They turned toward the center square and saw Father Zulemus still lingering nearby. They walked toward him, intending to brush past him, but then he stepped forward slightly and, as he did inside the pub, raised the cross of his rosary. "I see you!" he said, rasping over the words, as Kaper and Lukan skirted around him. And he pointed at them and twice said a word they'd not heard before, but one that fascinated them with its exotic lilt, and that word was *"Nosferatu!"*

TWENTY

aniel, still dazed by his time with Kasyn, walks the town's streets completely unsure of his purpose.

DANIEL WALKED the streets of the town center without direction, not sure why he was walking or what he was looking for, but he was sure he needed to be doing this instead of just going home. He saw several things and wondered if they were connected ...

...A lot of young kids wandering about. Not adolescents but true children, as young as maybe four years old. He didn't know if it was a school day or not. Maybe the school was closed because of the plague that everyone was ignoring. Maybe it was summer break. But still it was odd to see so many of them with no sign of any kind of adult supervision, and they seemed disoriented, lost, random in their bumbling progress through the streets.

...Father Zulemus walking rapidly down the street toward his church, head down and clutching his crucifix as if it were a shield. Daniel wondered what life would be like lived under such a dense cloak of delusion.

...Mayor Quode, Constable Snell and Doctor Micah entering his mother's infirmary, all three of them looking them tense, stressed, harried.

...Kaper and Lukan following two pretty boys whose names he couldn't recall into Kyban's diner. He thought to call out to them but decided to leave them to their fun. He needed the alone-time now anyway.

...And Gunna Quode, the Mayor's wife, approaching him quickly, wild-eyed, her hair a vast corona of strawberry frizz around her tiny, pinched face. She pointed at him and said, "Where has my husband gone?"

Finding this query to be very weird but seeing no reason not to answer it since he happened to know the answer, he pointed back toward the infirmary and told her that he'd seen the Mayor go in there a couple minutes earlier with Constable Snell. She shook her head and said, "That's what I thought you'd say. You've always been such a liar, Daniel Jasper." And she strode away. Bewildered, he wished he'd been able to think of a good retort to fling at Missus Quode, but the moment was gone.

What am I even doing? he wondered. *I'm tired. I need to go home.* He rounded a corner and headed out of the town center and toward his edge of Diaspar looking forward to a shower. He entered the narrow alley that passed between the wet market and the backs of the assorted shops of Orgone Street, the alley which eventually faded into the mulched trail that was Daniel's shortcut through Chasmanta Park to the bottom of Mircalla's hill where sat his house.

It was the lush center of the park, flush with cypress trees clung heavy with Spanish moss where Daniel started to sense that something was not quite right. Here a natural spring had centuries ago been tamed into a large marble fountain which fed a huge shallow pool inhabited by bronze and stone statues of mythical denizens of watery realms, and the burbling of the water was a constant sound here but so too was the chirping chittering racket of birds who regarded the water feature as a gigantic bird bath. During the daylight hours one heard the constant chatter of finches, robins, pigeons, doves, jays, thrushes, orioles, lorikeets; and at night one could expect the more eerie speech of owls and nightjars and florid vespertines and night herons and great potoos. Daniel realized that the sense of the uncanny came from the absence of the birds and their continual chatter. And then he saw why the birds had vacated the area: a huge panther trod across the width of the marble pool, winding its way among verdigrised statues, heading toward Daniel.

"Nox," said Daniel. He seated himself on the edge of the pool, dropped his feet into the water and let the huge cat approach. "We keep finding each other like this." He reached with both hands and clasped Nox's ears. The panther purred deeply, and Daniel wondered, "Does Kasyn know that you are here, that you are seeing me?"

Daniel somehow understood and trusted the sense of a request from Nox. He let the great cat rest his huge wet front paws on his shoulders and he leaned forward pressing his forehead against Nox's and he had the sensation of hearing this from inside his own head: *"Kasyn is terrified of you. When we arrived here, he had no idea that his entire plan would depend on you, Daniel. And he's afraid he can't control you."*

Daniel laughed. "He's fucking *right* about that. You want to tell him that, Nox?"

And Nox, a low rumble: *"In time, he'll figure it out for himself. I love Kasyn but he must learn the truth of you for himself."*

And the black cat broke the touch, backed away from Daniel, turned away and splashed out of the pool and ran into the cover of the trees.

TWENTY-ONE

Daniel recovers from his night in the crypt and is overcome with lust for Kaper and Lukan; he learns of the boys' new condition, and they share a revelation about himself; an unexpected arrival.

DANIEL HAD SPENT about a half hour in the shower periodically nearly dozing off under the hot spray. Eventually his tight muscles and scraped skin felt soothed enough and he stepped out and toweled off and examined himself in the mirror expecting to find numerous abrasions and little cuts and bruises all over his body after the ordeal with Kasyn in the crypt. But there were none. In fact, even little random freckles and sunspots that he'd always had were gone. His skin had never been smoother, freer of flaws.

Daniel pulled his fingers through his hair which felt silkier and thicker than ever, and he peered at his face in the mirror, expecting to see tired eyes but instead seeing a perfect complexion and brown eyes so shiny as to be almost glittery gold. And he suddenly felt extremely horny, so much so that pre-cum spontaneously streamed from his cock and he wondered where Kaper and Lukan were, wanting someone here for him to fuck as soon as possible. He gripped his cock intending to jerk off, but he released it almost immediately. *Later, later,* he told himself. The boys will be here soon, *their lean smooth bodies, bodies like Olympic swimmers, oversized nuts in tight smooth sacks, huge cocks dripping pre-jac, mouths full of hot spit, tight boy-cunts in between firm bulging ass cheeks*—and he had to take some deep breaths and make himself to take his hands off his cock and balls and try to calm himself down again.

Daniel pulled on a pair of white linen trunks and went to the kitchen. He turned on the television, which was showing *The Outer Limits* again, and he set to work preparing a martini. He hoped the blockade would end very soon because he was running low on dry vermouth and Thom Destrin didn't have much left at the pub either. He shook his concoction with ice and strained it into a huge coupe glass and dropped a blue cheese-stuffed olive into it.

The episode of *The Outer Limits,* already partway through, involved some ant-like creatures with creepy human-like faces who'd been exiled by their people to a desert on Earth which was being used by their race as a sort of penal colony for these creatures in exchange for giving Earth advanced alien technology. Watching the show while sipping his martini kept Daniel distracted somewhat from his aching nuts and stiff dick.

The show ended and another episode started, this one about a hapless pair of travelers whose car breaks down in a remote and desolated countryside and they come to be menaced by tumbleweeds that seem to operate with an unknowable and malevolent intelligence rather like the titular bushes in Blackwood's story "The Willows."

Daniel mixed another drink and wondered if he happened to have an emergency reserve of narcowhirl on hand. He climbed a stepladder to reach the very back of a high cabinet above his kitchen sink and he reached around for a little mason jar. Finding it, he brought it out and was happy to see inside it a glassine envelope filled with little rocks of the purplish glittery substance.

He went with this to the slab of black moonglass on his butcher block, tapped a few little chunks of the drug out onto it and took a pestle to it, crushing it to fine dust. With the razor edge of a vegetable cleaver, he pulled the dust into a narrow rail and, with a short copper straw, sucked it into his nose. He realized, of course, that dosing on this was at cross purposes with trying to keep his horniness under some measure of control as the initial thrill of the drug went straight to his balls, made his dick strain against the tight fabric of his shorts.

But it had another effect, too, one he couldn't recall having noticed before: everything alive now had some degree of shimmering aura about it. The house plants that festooned all his windowsills and which sat in rows of well-aged terra cotta pots in his back garden all shimmered now with a radiance that he'd never seen before. A pair of finches on the ledge outside the kitchen window glowed a peachy orange and one of the black feral cats that he kept fed groomed itself on the garden path and exuded a lustrous magenta flame. Daniel stepped out into the garden and looked east toward the forest and saw ranks of trees that seemed to burn with a citron heat. *Narcowhirl is not this kind of hallucinogen. That's not what's making me see this.* He went back inside, inhaled another line, wondered if this is how the world looked to Rhoda all the time. He flashed back upon his encounter with her the day before and her description of what she'd seen in his aura, of the dark thing cloaking him. It occurred to him to go to a mirror, and the idea made him briefly queasy. *No. No mirrors yet.* He picked up his drink and gulped the rest of it.

Daniel heard footsteps, still some distance away but approaching quickly, and very familiar in their gait: the boys were almost back. He sighed, sweaty with lust for them. A couple minutes later Kaper and Lukan passed through the garden and through the open kitchen door and Daniel wondered if they'd ever been more beautiful. Their auras were both hotly pink, but Kaper's flared and shifted toward violet from moment to moment while Lukan's shifted toward red. The scent of the pomade in their hair and of the sweat on their skin made Daniel's stomach nearly cramp with hunger. "Come here," he said, and the boys obeyed, arms outstretched.

He kissed them open-mouthed, one and then the other, Lukan and then Kaper, back and forth, slopping spit on their lips and chins. He lowered his head, turned his face upward toward Lukan and told the boy to spit in his mouth and he opened wide and Lukan dropped a heavy stream of drool between Daniel's teeth. Daniel pressed his mouth to Kaper's, fed him his brother's spit. He began to tug at the toggle buttons holding closed Kaper's vest and told the boy to strip. He unbuckled the clasp of Lukan's extremely short skirt. "Strip. Get naked, faggot. I want you naked." And he pressed his tongue into the boy's mouth while Lukan worked himself out of his clothing, and his tongue scraped against the new sharpness in Lukan's jaws, his nosferatu canines forced to full erection by the state of hot arousal that Daniel had put him in. Daniel pulled away and put a couple fingers in the youth's mouth, looked more closely, said "This is new."

Kaper, now naked as well, pressed up against Daniel and his brother and said, "I have them, too," and opened wide.

Lukan: "I didn't bite you, did I?"

"As if I'd mind," said Daniel, laughing, grabbing each brother by a wrist and leading them toward his bedroom. "Fuck now, talk later."

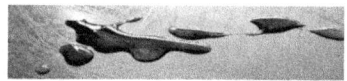

A couple minutes later, Kaper found himself at the center of attention with Daniel's mouth on his asshole, tongue massaging it while his cock was firmly in his brother's mouth, his thick oozing arrowhead fucked hard, wedged between Lukan's tonsils. He felt Daniel shift position, heard the snap of a cap—lube tube—and then Daniel's fingers on his asshole, pressing in, pre-lubing, and then and then and then the slick wet snapping sound of Daniel slathering his own cock with the gel and then another cap opened, and a vial raised to his nose—poppers. Kaper inhaled deeply, and a couple of times, and he felt the heat in his face and the peak of the rush as Daniel's thick cock penetrated him and he liked the familiar thickness that he hadn't had enough of lately. Getting fucked by Daniel was different than getting it from Lukan. Aside from their fuck-styles being different, Lukan's cock was a fair amount longer than Daniel's, but Daniel's was a lot thicker.

Daniel tried to take it slowly, tried to edge it. He didn't want to spill his load too soon, but he was so pent up. He ceased his thrusts into Kaper's body a few times, slowed the onset of his climax, resumed more slowly, nearly rode to the peak again and backed off again. But he couldn't maintain this for long and he realized during one deep push into the boy's ass that he was going to lose control, he was past the point of no return and so he pressed in as deeply as he could and emptied his cum into Kaper in a dozen spasms.

During this fuck Lukan had continued sucking and slurping on his brother's cock but hadn't made him spurt yet. He maneuvered his partners into a new configuration. Without explanation they understood what to do. Lukan lay on his back and Daniel straddled him, lowered his ass onto Lukan's cock, took it inside him. Kaper lubed his dick and knelt behind Daniel and between Lukan's legs and very carefully fucked into Daniel, his cock sliding against his brother's and together the boys double-dicked their lover until they both slammed their jizz deep inside him. The trio then separated and lay side by side for a little while and drifted through a short nap.

"And that's what happened, Daniel." Lukan sat down on the chaise next to him. After their nap, they'd showered and dressed and moved to the sitting room. "I don't think we would have *chosen* to do this necessarily."

"But it's like we *had* no choice really," Kaper said.

And Lukan, "It's like we were somehow *mesmerized* into it. Like we weren't at all scared and not all worried about what they'd do to us."

Kaper added, "And it sounds crazy to say it now, but it didn't hurt at all when they were ripping into us."

Lukan: "Right. It just felt like a really hot and dirty fuck." He leaned into Daniel a little bit, pressed a kiss onto his neck. "But with a lot more blood than usual, of course."

Daniel kissed Lukan on his forehead—so warm, but not sweaty. He hugged the boy tightly to his chest, tipped his chin up to Daniel's mouth, Lukan's hot wet mouth to Daniel's, and he slid his tongue between Lukan's lips, pushed a lot of spit onto Lukan's tongue, reached under the boy's short skirt and wrapped a fist around his stiff prick. Lukan pulled away from the deep wet kiss after a moment, laughing, telling Daniel to be careful. He opened his mouth wide and let Daniel see the new fangs that had again erupted in his jaw. "I haven't quite gotten used to kissing yet with these new teeth. They only pop in when I'm horny. And I don't want to cut your tongue. And I might have to re-learn how to give blowjobs."

Daniel swabbed fingers over Lukan's wet lips. "You can practice on me right now if you want." He grabbed Kaper by an elbow and pulled him closer. "Both of you. Take turns. You'll definitely know when you're doing it right."

Kaper laughed, pressed his mouth into Daniel's armpit and said—a bit muffled— "Are you seriously ready to go again already?"

"Absolutely." Daniel tugged open his fly, tugged out his cock. The brothers practiced their technique and before long sparred with their tongues over who got more of Daniel's spouting spunk.

Satisfied, chilled out, calm, Daniel settled himself against the back of the chaise. "I don't know how, but this seems somehow not all that surprising. It's almost like I knew as soon as I saw the two of you today that you'd be... different. It's like you have a new glow, like you're shinier somehow. And really beautiful. I mean, you guys have always been very pretty to look at and super-hot in bed, but it's more so now. Like you're really owning it somehow, like you know how fucking hot you are and it's showing through your skin."

Kaper got up and sat to Lukan's other side, leaned into his ear and whispered. But Daniel could hear him easily. He pretended he hadn't plainly heard Kaper ask, "Do you want to tell him how *he* looks now?" He pretended that he wasn't waiting for Lukan's answer. Daniel half-hoped that they'd drop the topic. *Do I really want to know what they're seeing?*

Kaper hopped up and stood in front of Daniel, hands outreached, and he told Daniel to stand up, which he did, clasping Kaper's fever-hot hands. Kaper looked at his brother. "You can see this, right?" Lukan affirmed it and Kaper said to Daniel, "You have wings, Daniel. Like a giant black hawk or eagle. It's like a black fire that cloaks you, like you're shining under a black sun. Did you know this? It's so pretty."

Daniel shook his head. "But Rhoda saw it. She wasn't as happy about it as you seem to be, to say the least. She thought it was an evil aura, or something demonic that I am dragging with me."

He noticed the boys sign at each other, exchanging some kind of secret, or maybe deciding what to say to Daniel next. Lukan said, "She didn't know what she was seeing. It frightened her. She doesn't know what we are now."

Daniel repeated those words slowly: "What...we...are... now." He shuddered, shook his head. "And I wonder what *that* means. Do you guys feel a great need to...maybe drink blood? Will you need that to live?"

Kaper and Lukan looked at each other, exchanged a few signs. Kaper said, "Not so much. I mean, we scarfed down some shawarma and beer at Kyban's a few hours ago. No real big craving for blood yet though."

Some noise outside made all three of them turn toward the front of the house. A car arriving? "Who's here?" Lukan wondered.

Daniel smiled. "Amazing. She's back already."

The twins said in chorus, "Your mother?"

Daniel nodded and said, "And she has brought someone with her. I can somehow hear that she has someone with her." He felt irrationally nervous, butterflies inside him, pointlessly afraid, unaccountably embarrassed. He addressed the boys: "Please stay back here for a bit. I may need a few moments to prepare them for...for what you guys are like now."

Kaper and Lukan smiled, shrugged, settled down on the chaise. Lukan reclined, laying his head in his brother's crotch. "We'll be good, Daniel."

"Daniel! Are you here?" His mother, the doctor, entered Daniel's house through the kitchen door. He rounded the corner from the back sitting room into the kitchen and stopped dead, unable to take another step until he was certain that he was seeing what he thought he was seeing.

Ezra stood in the doorway smiling. His face was almost a mirror of Daniel's though a decade older and he wore a thick mop of blond hair—a trait inherited from his biological father. His voice was a slightly deeper version of Daniel's, and he said, "Somebody's all grown up now."

Daniel rushed forward, pulled his brother into a tight

hug...and trembled. Ezra, whispering against Daniel's left ear said, "Don't cry. Or you'll make me cry, too."

Daniel laughed. "If you tell me not to cry, then I'll definitely cry. That's like telling someone who's afraid of dogs that they can sense your fear so you just need to not be afraid." He broke the hug and stepped back and took in a long look at his older brother. "I can't believe you're really here."

Ezra chuckled. "Honestly I can't believe it either." He glanced at their mother. "But it just sounded like too much fun to miss. A little nowhere town beset by a deadly plague and my little brother in the midst of it it—how could I say no?"

"Wait a minute..." Daniel looked at the clock on the wall and asked himself what day of the week it is and said, "How the hell did you get back here so fast?"

Elspeth laughed. "Well, all that was required to complete what you called my 'grand mission' to rescue our town from the plague, was to find a local doctor in Transovakia, explain our situation, get his help with lab tests on the samples that I'd brought and then have him send me to a real compounding pharmacy and hire them to make up a few thousand courses of an antibiotic capsule. So, I'd achieved all that before I'd been in town even a whole day. At some point the next morning I realized that I was famished, and, in a cafe, I happened to find this boy." She gestured broadly at Ezra.

Ezra nodded. "And I volunteered to do most of the driving so that she could get back here sooner and get in a nap on the way."

"And he is every bit as terrifying a driver as you are, Daniel, but I fell asleep before I could care too much."

Ezra grinned. "Which spared her seeing all the little

white crosses along the road marking where people had been killed in auto accidents."

"But I saw them on the way there!" Elspeth peered out the kitchen window. "That's quite a new neighbor you have up there. The Circus of Nights, I presume?"

Daniel considered carefully how to reply. "They're probably about to start tonight's show."

"Have you seen their show?" wondered Ezra.

Daniel nodded. "It's...something else." And he felt it before he saw it: the incoming presence of the Destrin twins.

Kaper and Lukan seemed to float above the floor a few inches and drift toward Ezra who backed up against the door, startled at this new thing in the world. Daniel spoke, his voice seeming to echo in the small room: "Stop, please. Give him some space. This is my brother."

The twins retreated, drifted backward and settled, feet on the floor, next to Daniel. Lukan smirked and stage-whispered, "But are we to have nothing tonight?"

Daniel stepped slowly toward his brother. "I feel terrible about this now. Ezra, you should not have come here."

"But you asked me to! In your letter." Ezra dropped his hands over Daniel's shoulders. "Honestly I was kind of touched that you wanted to see me." He pulled Daniel into a brief hug and said, "And whatever's going on here, I wouldn't miss it for the world."

Before Daniel could reply to the effect that Ezra should certainly want to miss what was going on there, he heard laughter from Kaper and Lukan. He turned around and saw his mother pressing her stethoscope against their chests, listening to Lukan and then Kaper and then back. Daniel said, "What are you doing, Mum? I don't know if messing around with them is a great idea right now."

"Daniel! How rude!" cried Lukan. "This is your own mother and our doctor. She is just giving us a proper check-up." He perpetrated a deeply dramatic flip of his loose bangs.

"This is definitely...weird." Elspeth said, "Their body temperatures are both 101.6F but they show no other signs of fever. Their blood circulates but I don't know how." She turned to face Daniel. "These boys have no heartbeat."

Daniel let that information hang there for a moment and then he said, "You're in a lot of danger here. Diaspar is under some kind of attack by this crazy troupe of circus performers and at least some of them are shape-shifting vampires. If you find this impossible to believe, then let me—"

Ezra cut him off. "We believe you, at least as far as them being dangerous. We know something about the Circus of Nights. We heard of some murders in Transovakia which locals were associating with some kind of circus. A woman who is a member of a cult called the Sisters of the Settled Hour said that one of their number had joined this circus a few years back."

Elspeth nodded. "We stopped for petrol in Keth, a town about halfway between here and the city, and the station was tended by a man who told us about this bizarre circus and how some of the performers seemed to transform into animals."

"Maybe that was just a stop on the way here," Daniel said. "This was their ultimate destination."

"But why?" Elspeth continued to peer at the twins, who in turn continued to smile at her.

"Their leader, Kasyn, is a cousin of the Baron Mircalla.

They're supposedly fulfilling a revenge curse that the Baron laid upon this town thirty years ago when the townspeople rose up against him and killed him. His curse supposedly decreed that all the children of this place must die as a prelude to his return to life."

"Madness," Elspeth said and, still watching the twins, "So, are *they*...vampires now?"

Daniel rounded the counter and clasped Kaper's head in his hands. "I guess maybe of some kind? Whatever has happened to them, they've definitely been changed somehow. They've both acquired a second set of canine teeth, which..." Daniel inserted a thumb and a finger into the boy's mouth and drew it open "...which appear when they get...aroused." *My hands on his body and my fingers in his mouth will do this for him.* "Look."

Elspeth gasped. "Amazing." She saw the new teeth somehow emerge from the boy's jaw, lengthening until they covered his normal canines. It resembled an effect in a film that she'd seen in which a man transformed into a werewolf over a series of juddering images.

One of Kaper's fangs cut into Daniel's thumb and he jerked away, further opening the cut. "Goddamnit." He was about to suck on the wound himself when he noticed a flash of gold in Kaper's eyes, and a low growl begin to rumble in his throat. "Seriously? You want this?" He offered to return his injured thumb to Kaper's mouth, but the boy burst with laughter and said he was just kidding.

Daniel said his mother, "You'll learn all the details soon enough from Doctor Micah, but you need to know that the circus has succeeded already in doing a lot of damage. There have been several murders of kids, and Micah thinks that they were killed by the kids' parents."

"What?" Elspeth took a step back from him. "Their parents!"

"I believe that the circus performance put into some people's heads a hypnotic conditioning that caused them to act like this. I swear I heard the lyric 'kill your kids' in a song that their band performed."

Ezra wondered, "But if you heard it, wouldn't others have heard it and wondered what the hell was going on?"

Daniel shook his head. "I may have been the only one who could hear it plainly."

Ezra frowned. "Why? Why you only?"

Daniel retreated a few steps from his mother and his brother. "There's something very *wrong* with me. I've been...perceiving things differently lately. And I've for some reason drawn the attention of the circus leader, that vampire named Kasyn. I...*fascinate* him somehow. Or he would have tried to kill me already."

"Kill you!" Elspeth said. "Why?"

"I'm one of the targets on their core hit list: a son of the doctor. Mircalla, with his curse, supposedly condemned the figures he most blamed for his doom and their children. Most of those people are already dead and gone, but equivalents still exist here. A doctor and her children. Ezra. *Fuck!* You're a target now, too, and I'm sorry! Also, the publican and his sons." He looked at Kaper and Lukan. "But they've been spared death, though they've been changed. Their father remains a target, as the son of one the men who slew Mircalla. Then there's the Mayor and his children, Lursa and Bethel. Mayor Quode was there thirty years ago, and the man who led the mob against Mircalla was the schoolmaster at the time. He's long dead, but they'll probably make Mister Marquist suffer for it. Also present for Mircalla's demise was an old priest named Maculus. He's long dead, too, and was replaced by Zulemus, who is now trying to sanctuary some kids in the church. Kasyn will want him dead, too."

"Wait," Elspeth said. "Why is Father Zulemus sheltering kids in the church?"

"They're afraid," said Ezra, "of their parents. Is that it?"

Daniel nodded. "I think that's exactly it. I saw a bunch of very young kids just wandering around downtown this afternoon. It was weird, but maybe that was why." To Elspeth he said, "Stay here with Kaper and Lukan. They will behave." He aimed his gaze at them. "Right?" Kaper smiled and Lukan drifted upward and executed a quick somersault near the ceiling.

The doctor, watching Lukan, said, "That's going to take a bit of getting used to." She looked at Daniel, and said, "I'll hang out with them. We'll get along just fine. But where are *you* going?"

"Eventually to the church. But first I want to try to find the Mayor and his daughters and get them to the church as well and any other kids or other likely targets for Kasyn we might find. Ezra, are you up for helping me?"

"Of course, but why there?" Ezra wondered.

"It's the most defensible place in the town. It sits high in what's basically a dead-end alley. There's really only one good way into it."

"And then only one way *out!*"

Daniel, adhering: "I know it's not great, but Zulemus and a bunch of the kids are there already. It will be simpler to make that the base than try to move all of them somewhere else at this hour."

Kaper bounced onto the kitchen island near Ezra and said to him, "I know this is a little off-topic, but you're just as cute as your brother. I wonder if you'd ever be interested in—"

"Stop," Daniel warned. "Leave him alone."

Kaper performed a spectacularly pouty face and said, "I was just *curious,* Daniel." Ezra smiled and blushed.

Daniel said to Elspeth, "Pretty much everybody in town is probably at the circus—tonight's show won't be done for a while yet. But maybe try to make some phone calls. If someone answers at Quode's house, tell them we're on the way there and that we want to escort them to the church. Try to call Mister Marquist and tell him to go there, too, if you can reach him, and your dad as well, Kaper and Lukan. And call Constable Snell and tell him what we're doing and to watch for circus people heading to the church, and to be aware that they are very dangerous."

Elspeth stepped closer to her son and gave him a look of great skepticism. "Why do you even think," Elspeth said, "that you can deal with all this by yourself?"

Daniel just looked at her for a few seconds as if he didn't hear the question. Eventually he said, "If I don't at least try then Kasyn and his crew are for sure going to murder every kid in this town. You have no idea how powerful these bastards are. But I matter to him for some reason. But I don't know why yet. If nothing else, I can distract him."

"Like you distracted the blockade guards the other day?" Elspeth said.

After a moment, baffled, Daniel said, "I don't think it's like *that* at all. What do you mean by that?"

Ezra and Elspeth traded very uncomfortable glances. Ezra said, "We stopped, expecting to have to negotiate our way into town. But the guards at that post are dead. Mum thinks they have been for a couple days, maybe since she left."

"I just…" Elspeth started, stopped, took a breath. "I just need to hear it from you, Daniel. You guys didn't do that, did you?"

Daniel, stunned, looked from his mother to Ezra to Kaper and Lukan and back to Elspeth. "What the fuck are you talking about? Are you seriously asking me if I murdered the blockade guards?"

Elspeth clasped her hands over her face and said, "Oh, thank god!" She looked up at him. "I just needed to hear *that* reaction from you, and I am so very sorry to have done that. It's just that everything is so goddamned weird here now that I needed to know for sure that you are still normal."

Daniel laughed rather humorlessly and said, "I don't feel *normal* at all, Mother, but I'm glad to have reassured you that I'm not going around town murdering people, for god's sake!" He paused, had another thought, said, "But if they've been dead since then, that means their night relief never came and discovered them. They would have been replaced, and soldiers probably would have been crawling all over this town trying to find out what happened. So that means that the cordon is down. People can leave town now if they need to." He glanced at the wall clock, squeezed Ezra's shoulder. "Let's go. Maybe we can make some progress before the circus ends."

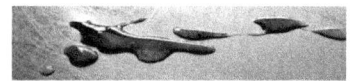

The brothers exchanged a long look at each other, turned toward Elspeth. Lukan said, "We're not *really* just going to stay here and let Daniel and Ezra have all the fun, are we?"

Elspeth smiled—just barely—at the boys and said, "Obviously not." She opened a drawer under the counter next to the refrigerator and withdrew a chunk of folded paper. "As *if* I'm letting those boys tell me what to do. They sometimes forget who their mother is." She unfolded the worn paper—an aged and ornate map of the town and its surrounding area—and spread it over the prep table. "We can work on this project, too." She pointed at a spot in the center of town. "This is the church, where they're trying to gather everyone. Daniel is not a hundred percent correct that there's only one way in." She pointed at the church and then to a building positioned slightly ahead of it in the alley. "This is the wax museum. Why the hell this tiny town has a goddamned wax museum of all things I will never understand, but here we are. Anyway, it shares a basement with the church because it's basically an annex of the church compound. I know this because Zulemus showed me around the whole area when I first came to town. If you can get into the museum from the back, over here in the next alley, you can go underground to a couple different flights of stairs that enter the church both from the front and the back. You could even come up into the church's atrium without needing to come through the front door."

Lukan said, "You're showing this to us like you think it's going to matter later."

Elspeth folded the map. "It might."

CHAPTER

TWENTY-TWO

Elspeth and the Destrin boys come upon a horrifying situation; an eerie automaton makes its move.

AFTER THE BOYS had packed themselves into the little car's back seat, Elspeth drove down Daniel's short driveway and onto the street that turned briefly back toward the hill of Mircalla's ruins and the glowing circus tent before bending again toward the town center. She abruptly mashed the brake pedal, stopping them cold in front of two figures that seemed to be dazedly crossing the street. The car's headlamps lit their startled faces when they turned fully to face Elspeth. She heard the boys in the back seat laugh. "What amazing luck!" said Kaper. "Just who we were looking for."

Elspeth was about to ask what he was talking about when she suddenly recognized Lursa and Bethel Quode, the mayor's daughters. The girls stood side by side, not really looking toward the car and making no move to get out of its way. The boys hopped out of the car and approached the

140

Quode girls. "Hey, what are you two doing out here?" Kaper wondered. He signed at Lukan, *Something's wrong with them.*

"I think we're going to the circus," Bethel said. "But I don't know for sure." Her voice was a drugged drone, like she'd maybe taken a lot of Benzedrine.

Kaper shook his head. "I don't think you should go to the circus tonight."

Lursa took an uncertain staggering step toward Kaper, and closer until her nose nearly touched the boy's. "I think our father tried to kill us."

"By locking us in the garage with the car running," Bethel added. "And then after we got out of there, we felt like we had to get to the circus."

"To find Daniel Jasper," said Lursa.

"To find Daniel?" Lukan peered closely at the girl, and more closely still as if trying to see something encoded in her glassy gaze. "What for?"

Bethel smiled slightly. "I'm not sure. It just felt like the right thing to do."

"Well, you're not wrong," Kaper said. "Finding Daniel's a good idea but he's not at the circus tonight." He glanced at Lukan, who nodded. "But we will take you to him. We're headed his way."

The boys directed the girls toward the car, asked them to get in the back seat. Lukan whispered to his brother, "It's funny how these bitches wouldn't go to prom with us, but now they—" And Lursa turned and slapped him across the face before getting into the car. Kaper laughed, jumped into the front passenger seat and invited his startled brother to sit on his lap.

Elspeth was about to take a left turn into Orgone Street and toward the town square when Lukan yelled, "Doctor Jasper! Stop here please!" He pointed toward a house set back a bit from the street. Lights were on, but the front windows appeared to be smashed, and the front door was off its hinges, lying in pieces of splintered wood and shards of glass on the front porch. "That's Auntie Rhoda's house. Something is wrong." Lukan flung open the car door, jumped off his brother's lap and ran toward the house. Kaper followed, ignoring Elspeth who was saying something about it being dangerous to just run in there, or something like that—the boys weren't really listening.

Elspeth told the girls to stay put and she ran after the boys. She passed through the empty door frame and into a room full enough of ornate clutter that it could have been an antique shop had many of the items not been carelessly knocked to the floor. She heard one of the boys yell *"no!"* three times, his voice tripping on a sob. In the very rear of the house, in a little room festooned with the tools of a psychic medium's trade, Kaper and Lukan stood to either side of a small table over which slumped the immobile form of an elderly woman. Kaper was quiet, tears flowing from his eyes. Lukan's eyes were dry but his face was hot and suffused with a dark rage. He said to Elspeth, "Daniel will kill them when he finds about this. *I* will fucking kill them!" He raised a hand toward Elspeth, clutching among his fingers a beaded leather choker. "This belongs to Dathan. They were here. Dathan and Chlora did this."

"Wait a minute." Elspeth rubbed her temples, trying to will away a brewing headache. "Who are Dathan and Chlora?"

Kaper's eyes were deep pools of unshed tears. "They're the vampires who turned us. Circus acrobats.

The boy—Dathan—wore that around his neck." His expression hardened, mirroring his brother's face of rage. "See how the clasps are busted? She didn't give up without a fight. Rhoda was kind of like family to us, and to Daniel. And to all the other weirdos and geeks and faggots that no one else much likes." He wiped his eyes with balled fists. "I can't even imagine telling Daniel about this."

Elspeth took a close look at Rhoda's corpse, trying to see any obvious signs of whatever trauma had killed her. *No blood anywhere.* Her face was nearly blue. Ligature marks around her neck. *Strangulation. Asphyxiation. Cardiac arrest.* "But why would they have done this? Why would Rhoda have mattered to them?"

Kaper looked at Elspeth miserably. "Maybe to try to get at Daniel? To *find* him maybe? She was a *real* psychic—I don't care what anyone else says. She could even do remote viewing. She may have been able to see where Daniel is, what he's doing, or what he *will* do in the future. And she refused to help them."

"But *what* do they need with Daniel?" Elspeth took a throw blanket from the back of a chair and draped it over Rhoda's body. "What's their purpose?"

Neither of the Destrin boys answered immediately, but Elspeth saw them exchange a series of hand-signs, and then Lukan spoke: "They're trying to resurrect Mircalla."

"*Mircalla?*" Elspeth sighed. "For god's sake, you guys, are you really still going—"

"*And,*" said Kaper, "they think that Daniel is somehow part of it. Like, he's either the key to it or maybe he stands in their way, but they need him for some reason."

"Jesus Christ, this is nuts." Elspeth tried to wish away the impending headache. She remembered that she had ibuprofen in her bag of meds in the boot of the car. "I guess, then, we need to—"

And she stopped speaking when she noticed a whirring clicking noise emanating from somewhere in the house and getting a bit louder and more distinct by the second. A shadow eclipsed the light between the kitchen and the middle room, and that shadow took a human form and moved into the kitchen and toward the meditation room. This was the source of the clicking and whirring. "Oh, fuck *me!*" Elspeth heard Lukan say. "Amazing!"

The shadow stepped into the light and Elspeth didn't know what to make of this new thing in the world. It looked like a mannequin from a clothing store, in the likeness of a square-jawed young man and dressed in a cricket uniform. It seemed to speak, and Elspeth parsed the sound as *"sussurus."* It looked directly at her with blue rollerball eyes and said it again.

Kaper stepped close to the thing and circled around it, fascinated. "His name is Choam. That's what Rhoda named him." The mannequin's head swiveled a few degrees toward Kaper and said, *"Choam."*

"But," said Lukan, "he didn't used to walk around or speak. This is new."

Elspeth sighed. "I guess this is not the *very* weirdest thing I've seen all day. What do you think it's...doing?"

Lukan: "I don't know why I'm feeling this, but I think he wants us to know something." He reached to his left, squeezed his brother's shoulder. "Maybe he wants us to know that he saw what happened to Rhoda."

The thing called Choam turned its head slightly to look directly at Lukan. *"Choam,"* it said. *"Knows. Saw."* And then Choam's eyeballs began to spin in their sockets, very fast, and they seemed to emit flickers of light. *"Saw,"* said Choam again.

"Hell yeah," Kaper said. "I think I know what he wants us to do." Kaper bent low beneath the kitchen prep block and found a big sheet of white butcher paper. "Turn off that light. Make it darker in here." Lukan did as asked and watched his brother warily, wondering what he was up to.

"Look at this." Kaper held the sheet of paper perpendicular to the floor and ceiling like a window screen or a curtain, a few feet in front of Choam's face, in front of his flashing eyes. A hazy juddering silver-and-black moving picture appeared on the sheet of paper. "He's showing us what he saw."

Elspeth watched, barely able to believe it, the repeating moving image of two lithe figures clad in skin-tight suits entering the front room, knocking things over and, before moving on to the next room, pausing to peer closely at Choam. "Are they Dathan and Chlora?" The boys nodded.

Choam produced an electronic whine that eventually started sounding like *"kill them"* again and again, and it turned toward the kitchen door and began to march from the room and back toward the front of the house.

"Shit!" Elspeth grabbed Lukan and Kaper each by a wrist and told them to get moving. "Come on. I forgot about Lursa and Bethel out in the car. If that Choam thing steps outside and heads toward them, they'll freak right the fuck out."

But, as it turned out, there was no danger of Choam freaking out those girls because they were no longer in the car.

CHAPTER

TWENTY-THREE

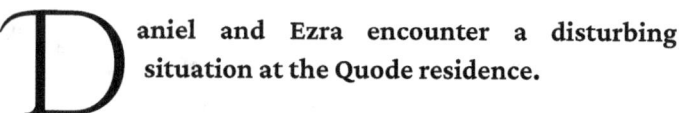

D aniel and Ezra encounter a disturbing situation at the Quode residence.

DANIEL AND EZRA stepped carefully through the front courtyard of Mayor Quode's home, taking this extra care because of all the overturned patio furniture and broken glass and trash and kudzu vines torn loose from the fence and the pergola. Beyond this disarray the house's large heavy oak double front door stood open which fact, to Daniel, was not a good sign. He grabbed Ezra by one arm when he felt like his brother was about to rush right into the house. "Hang on. Don't go in there. It doesn't feel right."

Ezra sighed. "What the hell does that even *mean,* Daniel? *Nothing* has felt right since we headed over here. *You* are acting weird as fuck, your boyfriends are levitating vampires and—" and Daniel pressed fingers to Ezra's mouth.

Daniel stepped closer to the open door and shouted. "Mayor Quode! It's Daniel and Ezra Jasper. Are you in there?" He took another step forward. "We're worried about you and your daughters. They are in a lot of danger right now!" He stepped into the doorframe and saw a long entry hall lit, barely, by a series of dim gas wall sconces. "Mayor! Are Lursa and Bethel here?" He felt Ezra close behind him. "Don't go in there," said Ezra, whispering. "Look. Down the hall."

Daniel saw movement at the end of the hall, an amorphous shape, a shadow, and then a dark form that rushed at him. He stood firm and the shadow-thing stopped and then stepped into better light and turned out to be Gunna Quode, the Mayor's wife, mother of Lursa and Bethel. She looked horrible, her small face a dark mottle of bruises, her long hair tugged into a cloud of frizz over her head. She reached one hand, finger pointed, toward Daniel and wondered, "Who are you? *Why* are you?"

"I'm Daniel, ma'am." He recalled his weird interaction with her on the street earlier that day when she definitely seemed to know who he was. "I was a couple years ahead of your daughters in school. Are they here now?"

And Missus Quode, her voice rustling like dry scraps of paper blowing down a dead street in a cold breeze: "Do what you want to me, but God will never help you. God turned his back on our world and he's not coming back, not for me, not for you, and not even to help my poor daughters."

Ezra stepped closer and said, "Where is your husband?" He reached toward the woman, as if perhaps to take her hand, but she revolted against this and shrieked. Ezra, undeterred: "Where is the Mayor? Where are your daughters?"

The woman issued a guttural chuckle and said, "It's been too late for all of us for a long time. My husband is dead. My daughters killed him. Or I think they did, anyway...yes, I think they did it with an electrical cord. Or maybe it was with...a series of satanic shapes." She shouted, pointing at Daniel, "And now *you* are here! *You* brought this to us! That's what the stupid priest said, that piece of shit Zulemus." She crossed herself and said, *"Be gone! Strigoi! Nosferatu!* Go back to Hell!"

Daniel, at once angrier, stepped closer, past the threshold, his advance seeming to repel the woman deeper into the hall. *"What* are you saying? What the hell do you even mean by that?"

Then Gunna Quode emitted a long low moan and took two steps closer to Daniel. She looked up into his eyes. "You were supposed to have been dead. You *were* dead." She heaved a great sob. "My husband killed you thirty years ago."

CHAPTER

TWENTY-FOUR

K aper and Lukan seek weapons among Rhoda's vast collection of curiosities; Kaper attempts to locate Daniel using an arcane method.

ELSPETH FELT MORE and more that she was just being dragged along by the Destrin boys, who had decided to go back into Rhoda's house to look for stuff in what they'd called an "inventory room." Lukan pushed open the room's heavy door, its bottom scraping against the wood floor. Elspeth asked again—because they'd ignored her the first time—what they were looking for in there. "Tools. Weapons," said Kaper.

"Weapons! For what?"

Lukan found a light switch, cast the room in the yellow gloom of a single huge overhead Edison bulb. "We will be going up against a gang of vampires." He looked at Elspeth, smiled. "We're kind of new at this shit but we know something about what they can do."

"Creatures that can levitate," said Kaper, opening an

armoire, "that have superhuman strength, that can turn into animals, that can maybe do other things we haven't even seen yet." He pulled a thick wooden crucifix from the cabinet, a luridly painted Jesus figure affixed to its front. He raised it to his brother's face. "These don't really do anything, do they?" He tossed the thing aside and brought out a heavy leather case. "I think this is it."

"Oh yeah," Lukan agreed, clearing space on a table for his brother to lay the case down and open it. It was filled with bolts—whole clips of them—for an antique repeating crossbow that Lukan and Kaper had found in a long-abandoned hunting lodge at the far west edge of the Spathe Woods. They'd brought it to Rhoda's house thinking for some reason that she might like to add it to her collection of curiosities. "But what did we do with the bow?" They'd hidden it somewhere because Rhoda had wanted them to get rid of it, fearful that the boys would hurt themselves or someone else with it, but they thought it was just too good to discard, so they'd discreetly tucked it away for later consideration.

"Top shelf." Kaper stepped over a box and a couple of ballroom chairs and opened a closet door as far as he could amid the clutter and reached up into its highest shelf, felt around for a moment, eventually withdrew the black metallic crossbow.

Lukan had found a big faceted crystal bottle of holy water with a silver cross affixed to its side. "Since holy crosses don't do anything, I bet this water doesn't either. If it did though, we could maybe spray the bolts with it and make them extra deadly to vampires."

"That would be sick as fuck, but I bet that water's just water. Here." Kaper reached toward Lukan with an open palm. "Drip some on my hand."

As expected, the holy water did nothing but get the boy's hand wet. "But maybe," Kaper said, "there's a way we can consecrate the bolts ourselves, with our own power."

Lukan understood his brother's proposal without any further explanation. He withdrew one of the bolts from the case and asked for his brother's hand and he dragged one razor edge of its head across Kaper's palm, cutting a deep gash. He spat heavily on the welling blood, handed the bolt to Kaper and offered his own hand. Kaper sliced open his brother's hand and spat upon it and then the brother's clasped their copiously bleeding hands together and dripped blood and spit heavily over all the crossbow bolts. "Vengeance for Rhoda," Kaper said. "Vengeance," Lukan repeated. "And love for Daniel," Kaper said. "Love," Lukan affirmed.

The blood flow stopped and the brother's unclasped their hands, pinkish with new flesh and nearly healed already. They realized that they'd forgotten about Elspeth who'd been standing back, watching them in quiet astonishment. She finally spoke: "You guys are straight up insane. But I don't have any better ideas right now. So, what's next?"

Lukan: "We must find Daniel now. Whatever Kasyn's plan is, Daniel is at the center of it. One way or another the rest of this night begins and ends with Daniel."

Kaper rubbed his temples, tugged at his hair. "Daniel and Ezra were planning to get some more of the town's kids to the church, including Lursa and Bethel. So, they could be anywhere in town. But I feel like they're either at the church already or..." he stopped, shuddered, suddenly chilled.

"Or..." Lukan, finished, "in the crypt?"

"It seems like that's where you'd go to finish resurrecting Mircalla, right? Assuming his remains are really still in that sarcophagus. We never tried to open it." Kaper looked at his brother. "If Rhoda were still with us, she'd be able to scry his location, either where he is now or where he will be soon. With a crystal ball." He sighed, looked down and away slightly, as if embarrassed. "She said I had an innate talent for it. I think I could at least try it." He resumed eye contact with Lukan. "I know you don't believe in any of this, but—"

Quickly, intensely, Lukan pulled his brother into a tight hug. "It doesn't matter. I believe *you*." He kissed Kaper on his forehead. "Let's try it."

Elspeth thought it was probably better that Kaper brought the crystal ball out from the meditation room and into the kitchen rather than try to use it right next to Rhoda's corpse. The ball, which rested on an irregular fuligin black trapezoid of stone, sparkled and flashed and seemed to hold within it a rotating cloud of glittering vapor. Elspeth helped Lukan light a bunch of candles and incense and found some markers and paper. Kaper said he might want Lukan to try to write down things that Kaper may say that he sees when he makes the attempt to use the ball. "I might see things that don't make sense at first. We might need to try to sort it out after." He looked at Lukan sadly, eyes glazed. "And I may not be able to do it at all."

Lukan clasped Kaper's hands and squeezed gently and told him that he'd do just fine and that it was at least worth a try.

Kaper seated himself at the kitchen table, took a deep

breath, clasped the sparkling globe in the long slender fingers of both his hands, lowered his forehead toward the ball, closed his eyes most of the way and...opened them again, sat up a bit higher and said this: "Their tent is coming down, collapsing like a cloud. This is happening now or will happen very soon. Makes sense. Tonight was supposed to be the final performance of the circus. That would be over by now. I see that giant kid—Jommy is his name—he's laying pieces of some kind of...glass in between layers of blankets. Yeah. It's the mirrors. They've taken down the hall of mirrors."

Lukan said, "That's right on top of the entrance to the crypt. I wonder if anyone is down there. Can you see it?"

Kaper took a deep breath, and seemed to shudder and then gasp, and then he said, "So cold in there now. They've taken the lid off the sarcophagus. They've opened the casket, and..." Kaper seemed to lose focus, his eyes rolled back a little bit and Lukan squeezed his shoulders and asked him what he was seeing and he came back to awareness and said this: "I'm not sure if this *will* happen or if it happened already. I think it's in the past. Earlier tonight. Mircalla's body is in the coffin but it's like a mummy, almost a skeleton even. Like he has no flesh. It's like skin stretched over bone, and there's a wooden stake through it —I guess that part of the legend is true. And they've set up a few galvanic lucifers to light up the space, but set very low, very dim, and they've cleared everything off our altar except the spirit board. They've set up new candles, lots of them, but they're not lit yet. It's like they've gotten ready for something but no one is there right now. The place is empty."

Lukan: "Where did they go? Where are they now?"

"Trying to see...trying to follow...a thread. It's *Kasyn* that keeps coming into my head, and Dathan and Chlora now. They were down in the crypt and then they went..." Kaper shouted a loud "fuck yeah!" and said: "It's amazing! I can see what they did, step by step. I'm following their path, like a glowing trail. They went to the church and they're in there now. And there are others in there with them. A bunch of the circus people...and kids, and that panther... And now...I see...Choam. But he's outside somewhere. In an alley. And it's like I can hear him *thinking*, searching, as if he's waiting for directions. Waiting for *us!* He's behind the church. Doctor Jasper, I think you may have been right that we needed to know about that back-alley entrance. He's just standing there...And now...and now it's Daniel and Ezra that I see. They're in the church now...I think. Or they will be there in just a few minutes. I'm also seeing them on the street outside. Not sure which has already happened." He pulled away from the crystal ball and stood. "We gotta go."

TWENTY-FIVE

Daniel and Ezra enter the church and confront Kasyn; Daniel again speaks to Nox and demands the release of the children.

IN THE ATRIUM of the church Daniel inhaled the ancient scent of this place where candles and incense had been burned continually for centuries. Candlelight flickered in the mirror-still surfaces of black-veined white marble ponds of holy water to either side of the entrance, and a low drone of atonal music from a bass and a theremin felt eerily out of place.

"It looks like we may have arrived a little late," Ezra said as they entered the main sanctuary of the church and saw what looked like a bunch of kids crowded into the gilt-domed apse of the church behind the altar, the stars of the circus lounging about the front of the chamber, the great panther patrolling the children's makeshift jail. Beyond the altar they saw what appeared to be a huge crucifix, inverted and with someone other than a Jesus figure attached to it, feet up and head down. "Oh shit," Daniel whispered. "That's Father Zulemus hanging there." Daniel grabbed Ezra's left shoulder. "Stop here. You don't have to go any further. In fact, you need to leave. Get to safety. This is my problem now."

Ezra sighed. "Fuck off, Daniel." Ezra walked ahead of him a couple of steps, turned back and whispered into his brother's ear. "You *know* I'm not leaving you here by yourself. And what the hell would I tell Mum anyway? 'Yeah, Mum, kiddo said he was just fine all by himself in the vampire murder church, so I figured I'd just leave him to it!' My god, she'd think we were *both* the biggest fools ever."

Daniel raised an eyebrow. "She may turn out to be correct in that supposition before this is over."

The brothers strode with purpose down the center aisle and Daniel called out to Kasyn with what he hoped was great vocal strength and a convincing tone of authority. "What's all this, Kasyn? Why are all these kids here?" The band stopped playing.

The ringmaster grinned and hopped upon the top edge of a pew, crouched there. "Oh, you know. We're just watching after them. All their parents seem to have gone missing. Or mad. Or dead. That weird priest was babysitting them earlier, but he certainly seems to have fallen down on the job." He pointed backward with a thumb toward the ghoulish crucifixion of Zulemus.

"I see." Daniel took three long steps toward Kasyn, stopping just a couple meters in front of him, looking him in the eyes. "You'll be letting them all go now."

Still smiling, Kasyn said, "Is that right?"

"That's right. You don't need them anymore. I'm here now."

Kasyn clapped his hands together and laughed. "Well!

You certainly seem to have an exalted opinion of yourself and your importance, young man."

Daniel stepped toward the altar and spoke to the panther. "You know me, Nox." The huge cat that is sometimes a man paused in his pacing and peered at Daniel, querying, uncertain. "We met in the woods, and we became friends, didn't we?" The giant black cat emitted the low rumble that was its purr. "And you visited me in the park, and we spent some more time together, didn't we?" Daniel crouched, eye level with the beast, spread his arms and said, *"Nox, come here."* And his voice seemed to reverb and echo in the chamber and the great cat obeyed him and approached Daniel and lowered his forehead to Daniel's.

"Incredible! Unexpected!" Kasyn said, delighted. "Absolutely savage! Do you see this, Magran? Did you hear that undertone in his voice? He can command Nox!" Magran watched the giant black cat yield to this bizarre human boy that seemed to fascinate Kasyn far too much, but she was much less impressed with this development than he was, and she said nothing about it.

Daniel stroked Nox behind his ears and under his chin and addressed the kids, "This big kitty won't hurt you. Not now. He's *my* friend now." He focused on a girl who seemed a bit older than most of this lot, a redhead in a purple jumper that he recognized from a summer school class that he'd tutored last year. "Your name is Robin. Is that right?" The girl nodded. "Okay, Robin, you are in command of these kids." He looked around among them and pointed out a boy perhaps close to Robin's age, a kid with an unruly mess of black hair and huge red-framed glasses. "Jarren, right?" The kid said yes, weakly. "Jarren, you are second in command. Your job is to help Robin get everyone out of here. Understood?"

"Yes, sir!" the kid said, drawing close to Robin.

Kasyn watched and clapped his hands to his cheeks and burst into laughter. "And I suppose I am just letting you do this, Daniel?"

"That's exactly what you're doing." Daniel had no idea how far he could push this but for some reason he felt like he could take it a couple steps further and he added, "I'm making the decisions now, Kasyn." And to Robin and Jarren: "Exit that way, to your right." He pointed toward the east transept. "There's a staircase in there that goes down to the basement. In the basement there's a hallway that goes to another stairway that goes up into the wax museum. Go out the back door of the wax museum and find somewhere to lay low. Stay away from adults, even your parents. *Especially* them. Until morning at least. This will be over by then. Go!" The children obeyed with appropriate haste.

Kasyn, still smiling, said, "Well, now you've really messed up my plan, Daniel. I hope you know that."

And Daniel: "You messed up mine by already being here when we arrived, so I guess we both need to adjust our expectations."

"Oh, we will." Kasyn rose from the floor and drifted backward toward the altar and seated himself upon it. "You especially, lovely boy, will be making some *major* adjustments."

CHAPTER

TWENTY-SIX

The boys encounter the librarian who has a startling insight.

KAPER AND LUKAN jumped out of the car on Orgone Street and told Elspeth to wait until the appointed time to come to the church with Lursa and Bethel whom they'd eventually found wandering in generally the correct direction. They'd made it one block down the street when someone approached, hailing them from across the street, and then dashing across it toward them.

Lukan signed something like "*This* guy? Really?" and Kaper nodded and said, "What's up, Chadon?"

The librarian pressed closer, clutching a sheaf of paper. "Do you guys know where Daniel is?"

Lukan answered. "We're on our way to him now. We think he's in the church by now."

Chadon nodded with vigor. "Yes, makes sense. Do you think the vampires are there as well?"

The boys, open-mouthed and startled, exchanged a brief glance and...

Lukan: *"You?"*

Kaper: *"Know?"*

Lukan: *"About?"*

Kaper: "The *vampires?"*

Chadon, saucer-eyed, sniffed: "I can inform you that I know all about them. And I know what they're doing. And how they're doing it."

Kaper looked at his brother, who shrugged and said, "And what exactly is that anyway?"

"They're trying to resurrect Mircalla, but the way they're doing it is incredibly ornate. It's a high order of dark art only possible from a supreme vampire witch, whom I believe to be either their mistress of ceremonies—that lady named Magran—or Kasyn, the one who does the act with the panther. What they're doing is a kind of sympathetic magic in which they are manipulating objects that represent people and ideas and forces. The circus is a central piece of it, a sort of black-magical axis. They're casting a spell with it. Or maybe another way to put it is that they're conducting a really elaborate seance. The acrobatics, the fireworks, the music, the band, the animal act, that fucked-up hall of mirrors—all of it contributes to the spellcasting. The most impressionable people leave the circus partially mesmerized and programmed...to do things which further advance the spell. Like murder their children or kill themselves."

Kaper said, "And all this shit somehow brings Mircalla back to life?"

"Sort of." Chadon took a deep shuddering breath. "It pulls his life-force back into the corporeal plane but...*listen:* he has no body anymore! His body's been decomposed in those ruins for decades. If he is to live again, he needs to take on a new physical form. Do you get what I'm saying?"

The brothers looked at each other, understanding what Chadon was saying, not really needing him to do what he did next which was to show them a piece of paper from his sheaf of documents. "This," said Chadon, "is the last known photograph of Mircalla. And I swear it has changed since just a few days ago."

Lukan looked at the photo and then signed closely, his hand inches from Kaper's eyes: *We need to get to Daniel now!*

CHAPTER
TWENTY-SEVEN

K asyn reprimands Dathan; a new persona starts to overlay Daniel's; Choam arrives on the scene; a tense stalemate begins.

DANIEL COULD TELL that Ezra was trying very hard not to react to the presence of Dathan and Chlora pressing in ever closer. "This one," said Dathan, "is absolutely bewitching. Look at those eyes. He's even prettier than his brother."

"Agreed," Chlora said, the word a gasp. "Those eyes are like wells. Kasyn, may we have this one, please?"

Kasyn stomped a foot hard on the marble floor. "Absolutely not! That you even have the nerve to ask right now astounds me." In one leap he jumped the distance over to the acrobats and pulled them away from Ezra. "The two of you will be on tight rations until further notice. Did you actually think I'd already forgotten about how I'd very specifically told you to feed those pretty twin boys to Mircalla's tomb and you instead just fucking *turned* them and *released* them! So now we have a pair of rogues running

162

around out of our control somewhere doing god knows what. You stupid fucks wear me out."

Kasyn turned away from them and walked a few paces back toward the altar and he was mildly startled when Dathan vaulted over him and landed in his path and said, "You're going to stop talking to us like that. We don't have to put up with it. We could take you down at any moment and you know it."

Kasyn grinned. "Oh? Is that right?" And, in a series of punches and kicks laid down too quickly for an observer to fully clock visually, Kasyn put the acrobat boy to the floor, leaving him crawling back toward his sister, gasping and crying.

"Stop this!" Magran shouted. "I cannot stand any more of this nonsense with the two of you."

Kasyn shrugged. "He'll be fine in a few minutes. His young bones always knit quickly."

Daniel stepped closer to Magran and caught her gaze and leaned in a little closer, whispered, "This is quite a messy little family you've created for yourself...Juyann."

It was obvious to Daniel that Magran tried very hard not to react to his use of that name but after a few seconds she said, "You don't know anything about the person who used to go by that name."

Daniel smiled coldly and Magran backed away a couple steps and he said in a voice that was someone else's, *"I know all about you, faithful Juyann."*

Stunned, said Magran, "It's really you. I dared not believe it."

Kasyn drew close to Daniel and said to *Mircalla*, "Can you hear me, cousin? Should we move to the crypt? Is it time to move to the crypt?"

Daniel in the other-voice said, *"That may not be neces-*

sary. I find that I gain strength over the will of this boy minute by minute. It's a fine body that you happened to find for me. But he found his way to me, didn't he, cousin?"

Kasyn lowered his gaze as if embarrassed. "It would seem so." Kasyn peered more closely at Daniel/Mircalla. After a couple moments, he said, "I still see Daniel's aura dominant and flaring. He has not surrendered yet, Mircalla. Not even close."

The Mircalla voice emitted a low chuckle. "In time, Kasyn. I feel his will beginning to collapse brick by brick. In a short time, there will be nothing left of him."

A voice, like Daniel's but not: "That's not true! He's stronger than you know!" said Ezra.

Kasyn considered Daniel's brother with an expression of sadness dimpling his face and he said, "I understand your belief in him, and it's touching to hear it expressed so earnestly by his brother, but you have no idea of the power that is at work here. Mircalla was destroyed thirty years ago and yet he speaks to us now. This has never happened before. He may be the most powerful of our kind that has ever existed. As unique as your brother is, he is still just a human boy."

"Just a human boy," said Daniel—really Daniel this time— "who's going to wreck your plans before this night is over. I am not giving myself up for this. I don't care how first of a kind it is."

Kasyn was about to reply when his attention was captured by the sound of a weird mechanical whirring and clicking coming from somewhere within the chamber, echoing loudly throughout it.

Chlora tapped her already-recovered brother's shoulder. "Look." She pointed down the long aisle toward the church's atrium, toward a figure that was slowly marching into the sanctuary.

"How the hell did that thing get here?" Dathan wondered. It was that weird mannequin or automaton from the home of the witch.

Chlora took a few long strides down the aisle toward the mannequin. "Hello? How did you get here? Are you looking for someone?"

The artificial boy emitted a piercing mechanical whine and then another sound beneath it that was plainly a word: *"Looking."* And: *"Looking for you."*

Chlora probably didn't really know what exactly happened to her. She may have detected the automaton raise an arm, may have registered that it held some kind of device, may even have started to hear Dathan yell "Chlora, be careful! He has a—!" But before her brother could finish the warning, she had three crossbow bolts in her chest, two of them pierced all the way through and jutting out of her back.

"No!" Dathan fell into screaming sobs. Kasyn and Magran looked on in cold astonishment. Chlora spun and tottered, tried to grasp the bolts, and it seemed that she even tried to shape-shift in a panicked effort to dislodge them. For barely a moment she became a black vapor, but instantly collapsed back into corporeal form, dropped to her knees and then to her back and then burst into flames, a fire so hot that she was totally incinerated in seconds.

And then Dathan dropped to his knees and started to die. Kasyn looked at Magran, baffled. "Oh, my sweet son." She brushed tears from her eyes. "Their bond is total," she said to Kasyn. "One cannot live without the other. Literally. They were born this way. There's nothing I can do for him."

Kasyn gaped at her, appalled. "Madness. That's ridiculous. Let me try something. I'll give him some blood." Kasyn rushed to the stricken boy, but then backed away as hot white smoke began to pipe from Dathan's body. He shouted at the mannequin, "But you're not alive!" He turned a full circle as if trying to see something hidden somewhere in the dark recesses of the chamber. "This thing has no life-force. It's dead! So who controls it?"

A voice, or voices combined as one, echoed in the chamber. *"We do."* And then Kasyn marveled at this sight, at this new thing in the world: emergent from the gloom of the atrium and gliding down the center aisle a few feet above the floor came the raven-like forms of two black-clad vampire youths. "We do," they said again and drifted past the mannequin and over the ashen remains of Chlora. Dathan, now burning from within, skin falling away as ash looked up at Lukan and Kaper and said, gasping, "We gave you our *love!* And you did *this* to us!"

Lukan, still aloft, turned toward Dathan. "Get fucked, you dirty son of a bitch!" He spun in the air and with both feet kicked hard the disintegrating vampire's head, which cracked and exploded into dust and blackened bone fragments. "That's for Rhoda, you piece of shit!" The remainder of Dathan's headless body collapsed to the floor and dissolved suddenly into the same grey ash that was all that remained of his sister.

Kaper and Lukan settled, feet on the floor, a few meters in front of Daniel who looked at them wide-eyed, mouth agape, and said, "What the fuck are you guys doing here? You were supposed to have stayed at the house. You were supposed to have stayed safe!"

Kaper leaned toward Lukan's ear and stage-whispered, "Obviously he wasn't as impressed with our entrance as we'd expected."

Lukan said, "You're out way past curfew, young man, and I don't like the look of this crowd that you've fallen in with. We've come to bring you home. You ready to leave?" Behind him, Choam ejected the spent crossbow clip and loaded another.

Daniel's eyes shined with unshed tears and he said, "It's not going to be that easy, babe. We're not quite done here."

Kasyn stepped up beside Daniel. "No, we most assuredly are not. But you two pretty lads are done with your little reign of murder here. Observe." He pointed toward Ezra who was now being held in an armlock by one of the band members, with a knife to his throat. "And look back there." He pointed down the center aisle toward the atrium, and the twins turned to see Elspeth, schoolmaster Kellan Marquist, Chadon Lyndron and the Quode sisters being led into the chamber by a small gang of circus personnel including the giant Jommy and the little clown. Kasyn, addressing Kaper and Lukan, continued, "I can't seem to figure out how to break your psionic control over that...*robot* or whatever the hell that thing is that has the crossbow, but I'm willing to bet that you won't use it again if I hold forfeit these lives as your payback for any further attack upon my people." Kasyn stepped very close to the boys and said softly, "I need to be very honest and confess something: I think that you two are absolutely magnificent —the most exciting creatures I've seen in years—and I hope that you will join my circus after all this blows over. But until then, know that if you make that thing fire one more bolt at any of us, I will have all these humans killed."

Kaper, not removing his glare from Kasyn, said, "Choam, stand down." The automaton whirred and clicked and lowered the arm holding the crossbow, but he did not let go of it.

TWENTY-EIGHT

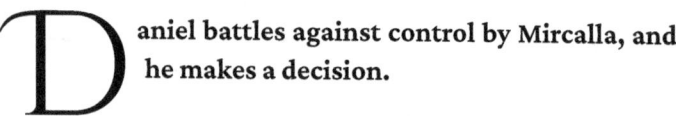

Daniel battles against control by Mircalla, and he makes a decision.

AN HOUR PASSED in an excruciating stalemate as Mircalla and Daniel struggled for control of the same body minute by minute while Kasyn's thugs held their hostages. Kaper and Lukan could see the competing auras surrounding Daniel's body. The phantom aura solidified again and the other-voice reasserted itself and said, *"I am very close to you now, cousin. I just need to work a little bit more to dissolve the boy's persona. He is so strong, but he is now, finally, weakening quickly. A first blood meal will help. Bring me his pretty brother, Kasyn."*

Kasyn strode toward Ezra but stopped abruptly, felt himself be lifted slightly from the floor and dragged back to where he'd been standing originally. Startled, Kasyn wondered, "Who did that?"

"I did," said Daniel, back again, speaking in his own voice.

Magran whispered to Kasyn, "This is dangerous. If Daniel can retain his identity but wield Mircalla's power, then he'll be able to—"

"But he won't!" And that was Mircalla again, through Daniel's throat and mouth. *"He dies a bit more every moment."*

Lukan stepped close to Daniel, grabbed his hands. "Daniel, listen to me! You are stronger than Mircalla. You can stop this now. Don't let them do this to you!"

The Mircalla-thing twisted Daniel's grin and warped his voice. *"Stupid kid. You'll look so pretty, naked and dead in my bed."*

"Fuck you!" Lukan slapped Daniel's face, tears streamed down his own. "I'm not talking to *you!* I'm talking to my friend. Daniel, please hear me!"

Daniel suddenly clasped his arms around Lukan. He was back at least for the moment. "I hear you, babe. Now you have to listen to me. Step away from me. Get back. You need to get away from me."

"No, goddamnit! I need to stay right here and—"

"Lukan! Listen to me. I love you so much, but you need to get the hell away from me. This is very dangerous. I'm getting weaker. Time is running out."

Daniel raised a hand and gave the boy an invisible nudge and Lukan drifted several meters back toward Kaper.

Daniel called to his family. "Mum. Ezra. Whatever happens, know that I love you and I have no regrets. I've already seen the other side and I have no fear." And to the Destrin boys: "You know and I know that our love can't die." And then Daniel said, "Kasyn, I'm not letting that bastard live again." He closed his eyes and said one last thing: *"Choam, help me."*

Kaper was the first to understand what was happening and, later on, the others would recall most clearly his blood-chilling scream of *"No!"* and his too-late lunge at the automaton, flying into it and knocking it over, as the beginning of the several minutes of mayhem that followed.

But Daniel... *no!* Kaper screamed, and...

...but Daniel...

...was pierced by several crossbow bolts, and...

... *"No!"* and Kaper toppled the automaton a second too late, and Daniel...

... *"No!"* the boy screamed, grabbing at the crossbow...

...then seemed to turn into a rotating, twisting pillar of blue flame...

...And Kaper: *"Goddamnit, no!"* and he grabbed at the crossbow...

...of blue flame that rose briefly nearly to the apex of the church's high vault...

And Kaper screamed and took the weapon from Choam's hands and—

... rose briefly nearly to the apex of the church's high vault before collapsing in an instant to nothing but a mound of ash on the marble floor...

And Kaper screamed and...

...to nothing but a mound of ash on the marble floor...

And Kaper shouted, his voice booming like the choir of Hell raised into the church, *"This didn't have to happen!"* and he reloaded the crossbow and fired at the thug who'd been holding Ezra, piercing his skull, sending the creature reeling and falling to ashes. He shouted at Elspeth and the Quode girls and Chadon to drop to the floor and he fired at the giant Jommy and the diminutive clown and lit them both up.

Lukan picked up a dropped knife and corkscrewed through the air at the remaining three members of the band who were now trying to flee down the center aisle, and he slashed their throats to the bone and their heads crumbled to ash.

Kaper reloaded the crossbow and turned it against Kasyn and Magran and fired several bolts but they each evaded his shots by briefly blinking out of existence—or that's how it looked to everyone else.

Kasyn spoke to the panther: "Nox, it looks like it's time for us to go. Meet at the rendezvous point." The great cat fled the chamber, dashing down the center aisle and out the front of the church. Neither Kaper nor Lukan tried to impede his departure.

Kasyn and Magran, standing in front of the altar, joined hands as if they were a diabolical bride and groom. Said Kasyn to Kaper and Lukan, "You kids ruined everything, you know. Pray that we are somehow able to forget about you, and that you never see us again." And the pair seemed to disintegrate first into fog and then into a cloud of roiling insects twisting like a cyclone and then into nothing at all.

EPILOGUE

The Destrin brothers stood behind Daniel's house —*their* house now, per Elspeth—and watched the small bustle of activity on the hillside. Three trucks and a few men from a construction company from a nearby town that their father knew had spent much of the morning preparing for what they'd called a "controlled implosion."

Kaper pulled a little jar from his pocket, nudged his brother, shook the jar. Eight sharp teeth rattled inside it. There'd only been four earlier that morning. "They just kind of popped out when I was in the shower."

Lukan smiled, kissed Kaper's cheek, said, "Can you still levitate?"

"No." Kaper laughed. "Honestly that's the one thing about it that I kind of wish we could have kept."

"Same." Lukan pointed toward the hill. "It looks like they're about to do something." In the distance they could see and hear a man speak into a megaphone though they couldn't make out what he was saying.

There wasn't much noise, but the ground shook for a

couple seconds and then a cloud of dust seemed to rise like a black fog above the hill, one side of which was now noticeably lower.

Every trace of the circus had vanished almost as quickly as its ringleaders had from the church that night, evanescing almost as impossibly as it had appeared in the first place, and probably no one in this little town would ever have to worry about vampires again, but the boys wanted to make sure that if Kasyn and Magran did ever decide to come back there and try again to raise Mircalla they'd have one fuck of a time getting at his crypt now that it was buried under thousands of tons of collapsed earth.

And it wasn't just that the circus was gone without a trace, it seemed to the Destrin brothers that the entirety of recent events was somehow fading from the memory of the town already. Funerals happened, children and some adults were buried, the plague ended, and no one really talked that much about how or why so much death had been visited so quickly upon the little town. It was almost as if when the circus vanished from the hill it took with it not just the memory of its presence but the memory of everything else that had happened around it.

Kaper recalled the awkward wake for Daniel that they'd held at their father's pub and how people had struggled to know how to express condolences, maybe because hardly anyone knew what had actually happened to Daniel. It was hard to explain it to anyone who wasn't in the church that night without sounding absolutely mad. He remembered Chadon approaching shyly, eyes downcast and with something in his hand that he offered to Kaper. It was a paper card with bibliographic information for a book. "I lent Daniel this book recently," the librarian had said. "It's probably in his house. This is its catalog card. You guys should keep it. The book. I don't want to check it into the library." To Kaper and Lukan it had been such an odd gesture, but they'd understood that this was Chadon doing his best to tell them that he mourned, too, and that he grieved for them, too, and they'd each thanked him and hugged him for a few long moments.

They'd had more awkwardness with Ezra who'd told them at the wake that he was soon off to the Dutch Argentine where he had some relatives. He'd said that he was going to run a beach bar there and that Elspeth might join him as well "After she feels that Micah can take over her practice here. So maybe never. But how about you guys come? At least for a while. What's there for you to do here anyway?" After a pause, he'd added, "And listen, I'm *not* trying to replace Daniel for you!"

Lukan's reply: "Well, there's at least *one* way in which I don't think you ever could, and I don't suspect you'd even want to try." And this had made Ezra blush.

Kaper shook these memories out of his focus and scratched the tips of his fingers down Lukan's back. "Walk with me for a little while?"

Lukan nodded and they wandered toward the edge of the Spathe Woods, thinking they'd linger by the creek. After a while, Kaper said, "You know, I really think Daniel *said* something to me—like right at the end. Straight into my head, I mean."

Lukan surprised his brother by saying, "I know. Me too."

"Really? What did he say to you?"

Lukan shook his head. "I'd rather not try to repeat it. Not now anyway. Not today. It will make me cry and I'm sick of crying every five minutes." The funeral had just been the day before. They didn't know yet what to do with the little metal box of ashes they'd kept, that they felt they should keep. Lukan nudged his brother. "But you can tell me yours if you want."

Kaper took a breath and then a deeper one and, "He said that he will see us on the other side. He said that he had already been able to see ahead, and he knew this for sure and that's why he wasn't afraid to go. He said that it will be a hundred years for us, but it will feel like no time at all for him, and that we always need to be good to each other."

They walked quietly for a few minutes under the moss-cloaked trees, approaching the creek. Eventually Lukan said, "Same. I mean, what he said to me sounded a lot like that." Kaper smiled, nodded, happy to hear this. And then Lukan added, "But he said one other thing, too."

Kaper stopped walking. "What one other thing?"

Lukan, smiling crookedly: "Well, I think he meant for me not to tell you this, but...he said that he always thought that I was just slightly the cuter one." He backed away from his brother, as if he might need to run for safety.

"You motherfucker." Kaper lunged, and Lukan took off down the path, and they ran, laughing until they reached the creek and Lukan tripped on a tree root and he went down in the water and his brother fell upon him and they lay there together in the shallow stream in a tight hug for a couple minutes, and a couple more minutes because Kaper felt his brother tremble and try to hold back tears until he couldn't, and Kaper just held him and he didn't feel he needed to say...

...*It's okay*...

...*It's okay—we went through some crazy stuff*...

...*some really fucked-up shit*...

...*And we lost Daniel*...

175

...because they'd said these things to each other a lot of times already in the days since that night in the church.

Eventually Lukan's tears subsided and he pulled away from Kaper a little bit and tried to smile, and they just sat there in the water and mud looking at each other for a few moments until they heard the crisp crackle of dry twigs breaking nearby, the crunching of fallen leaves. They sat up higher, then rose to their knees, looked around. More twigs snapping, leaves rustling, and then a low and warm rumble very nearby. The boys very slowly turned around and beheld just a few yards away a shining obsidian beast watching them.

Together they said, "Hey, kitty."

—Saint Louis, October 2024